Farley is only nineteen and has no idea what to do with his life. That wouldn't be a problem if he hadn't found his mate, but he has, and he wants to protect Irwin with everything he has.

The problem is that he doesn't have much.

Irwin has been under his mother's thumb all his life and doesn't know how to get away. He's sure everyone in the pride knows how abusive she is, yet no one has ever tried to help.

Until Farley entered his life.

Irwin has never fought back, but now he has a reason to. He wants a future with Farley, even though neither of them knows what that future will be like. The problem is that his mother won't relinquish her control over him easily.

But Irwin isn't alone anymore, and he and Farley are ready to fight.

Farley
Copyright © 2023 Catherine Lievens
ISBN: 978-1-4874-4007-7
Cover art by Angela Waters

Published by eXtasy Books Inc

Look for us online at:
www.eXtasybooks.com

FARLEY
GREEN HILL PRIDE 9

BY

CATHERINE LIEVENS

CHAPTER ONE

Farley didn't know very many people at the party, but he wouldn't have missed it for anything. Jordan might not be his best friend, but he was part of the group of friends Farley and Miko had made recently, and he loved that it wasn't just the two of them anymore.

Besides, he'd always been curious about the pride. Every supernatural creature in town knew about them, but they'd always kept to themselves. They'd been a mystery until their alpha had changed, and now that they were more open, everyone wanted to take a look.

That included Farley. He hadn't been sure what to expect from the pride and the house they lived in, but he'd been a bit disappointed when he'd realized they were normal people who lived in a normal place. Everything about them was normal, which was probably a good thing. A bit boring, but then, life in Green Hill was usually boring.

He grabbed a drink and told himself he needed to step away from the food table. He looked like he was propping it up. Usually, when he went to parties, he stuck by Miko's side. They'd been best friends since they were children and had always been there for each other. Now, Miko had a mate, which meant that he spent more time with Robin than with Farley. Farley wasn't jealous, but he missed his friend.

He looked around, trying to find Miko. He couldn't see him anywhere, but there were a lot of people in the room, so he was probably there. Farley had already seen Miko's uncle and his mate, and for a moment, he was tempted to find them.

"Hey," Jordan said as he appeared next to Farley. He grabbed an empty plastic cup and filled it with water. "What are you doing hiding back here?"

Farley raised his cup. "The same thing you are."

Jordan grinned. "I'm glad you came."

"I'm glad I came, too. You know a lot of people."

Jordan chuckled. "Most of these people belong to the pride. I've known them since I was a kid, so they kind of had to be here."

"I don't think anyone would be here if they didn't want to be."

"You're probably right. Anne was pissed when she realized I was having a party and didn't ask her to cook."

Farley didn't know who Anne was, but his curiosity about the pride was still very much a thing, so maybe Jordan would give him some details. "Who's that?"

Jordan shrugged one shoulder. "A pride member. Not one of the good ones."

"I see. And she's in charge of the cooking?"

"Yeah. She put herself in charge, and it's been that way for a while. I was hoping things would change now that Gal is the alpha, but she's still the queen of the kitchen. Thankfully, she knows better than to start trouble when she doesn't get what she wants, but I wouldn't be surprised if she still found a way to make me pay for not asking her to cook."

Maybe it was for the best that Farley and his parents had never lived in a Nix village. It wouldn't have been the same thing, because Nix had their own homes and didn't live in a group in a big mansion, but they did have to follow the leader's orders, and like any other group, there was a hierarchy in the tribes.

Farley's parents had left their tribes when they'd met. Their people hadn't been happy about them being mates because they didn't belong to the same tribe, and back then, there'd been no law against preventing mates from being together. They'd chosen each other rather than their families, and thankfully, they'd found Green Hill. The fact that they weren't the only Nix couple who had to go through that showed that Nix were just like shifters and other paranormal creatures when it came to their traditions. Things were changing, but it was slow going.

Farley didn't have to worry about any of that. He'd lived in Green Hill all his life and had no intention of leaving. Many of the people he and Miko had graduated with had left for college, but Farley still didn't know what he wanted to do with his life. The only thing he was sure of was that he didn't want to leave Green Hill, but that wasn't as helpful as he wished.

"Well, if you need any help with her, you just have to call," Farley said.

"She's not going to attack me or anything like that."

"I didn't think she would."

Although maybe he should have. She had to be a tiger shifter like Jordan, and he could imagine how much damage they could do to each other when they shifted. He hoped Jordan wouldn't have to deal with that. He'd offered to help, but he doubted there was anything he would be able to do if there was a physical fight.

"Thanks for the offer, but if she gives me any trouble, I'll go to Gal."

"You think she'll listen to him?" He might be their new alpha, but it was clear he still didn't have everything under control.

"She doesn't listen to anyone, not even her son. Honestly, though, I don't care. She probably won't be able to reach me anyway. I don't live here anymore."

He'd moved out recently. It was something Farley had been thinking about doing, too, but he was only nineteen and was fine staying at home. His parents were making noise about him finding a job, and he was fine with that. He just wasn't sure what kind of job he could find, but he was looking, and once he found something, he had every intention of helping his parents with the bills. He was an adult now, and while he wasn't planning on getting his own place because he didn't need it just yet, he didn't want to be a burden.

Jordan threw away his cup and clasped Farley's shoulder. "I'm going to find Nestor."

"I haven't seen him yet, so say *hi* for me."

Jordan nodded and disappeared into the crowd. Farley followed his path for a moment, which was the only reason he saw the man standing against the wall by the door.

For a moment, his brain couldn't understand what he was seeing. The man's brown hair was long enough to almost cover his eyes, as if he was using it to hide. His gaze kept bouncing around, and his body language told Farley that he was ready to bolt. He looked almost afraid, which didn't make sense, since this was a birthday party.

Why would Farley's mate be afraid?

That was the other part Farley couldn't make sense of. He reached back, trying to find the table so he could keep himself upright, because his legs felt like jelly. He and Miko had joked about him finding his mate since Miko and many of their friends had, but Farley hadn't believed it would happen anytime soon. What would be the odds? There were already so many people finding their mates around here, and Farley had never been that lucky.

It looked like he'd been wrong.

He didn't know what to do, so he did what his instincts told him. He pushed away from the table, moved toward the wall, and crouched behind another smaller table. Thankfully, there was no one here to watch him freak out. He pressed his back against the wall and tried to breathe, which was easier now that he was sure his mate wouldn't see him. The man wasn't a Nix, so he wouldn't know who Farley was just by looking at him, but there was a good chance he was a shifter. That meant he'd smell their bond if Farley went anywhere near him.

So Farley stayed where he was and tried to make sense of what had just happened. Unfortunately for him, his brain seemed to be frozen, and he still hadn't wrapped his mind around all of it by the time Thedric found him.

"Farley?" Thedric asked.

He sounded worried, which, considering Farley's position, made sense. Thedric was Miko's uncle, and while Miko and Thedric hadn't talked much in the past, they were close now. Thedric had recently told his parents to fuck off when they'd tried to force him to stay married to his wife even though he'd met his mate, and Farley had been in awe of how strong the man was. He wasn't sure how he felt about Thedric, of all people, finding him in this position, but there was no going back. Besides, considering how close Miko and Farley were, Thedric probably saw Farley as another nephew. He'd take care of him.

Farley looked up at him. "I saw him." He realized it didn't make much sense, but Thedric spoke before he could explain himself better.

"Saw who? Miko? He was looking for you."

Farley shook his head. "Not him. My mate. I saw my mate."

And he didn't know what the fuck he was supposed to do about it.

Irwin stayed close to the door in case he needed to run. Being here was a bad idea, probably the worst idea he'd ever had, but he hadn't been able to resist. Besides, he wasn't the only pride member here. Jordan had been vocal about inviting whoever wanted to come, and that included Irwin.

He bit his lower lip. No, it didn't include him. He and Jordan weren't friends. If Jordan saw him, he'd probably kick him out, but that would be fine. That wasn't what Irwin was afraid of.

No, he was afraid of his mother.

This party was a pride thing, but his mother had been adamant that he couldn't go. She'd ranted about Jordan not wanting to have her cook for it. Then once she'd found out that Jordan had invited people from the outside, it was about them invading pride territory and the house. Irwin found it ridiculous. It wasn't like they were at war and these people were going to kick them out of their home. They were just friends and family, wanting to celebrate someone's birthday.

Irwin hadn't expected Jordan to have so many friends. Most of them weren't even shifters, and they definitely weren't tiger shifters. That was another thing Irwin's mother hated. As far as she was concerned, tiger shifters should stick with tiger shifters. They didn't have any reason to be with any other kind of people, which was stupid, although Irwin would never have dared tell his mother that. Jordan's mate wasn't a tiger shifter. What was Jordan supposed to have done when he realized that? Leave him behind? It wouldn't have been fair, and even though Irwin didn't know Jordan's mate beyond seeing him around the house a few times, he was glad Jordan had stuck with him.

Jordan was a nice guy, as were most of the people who lived here. Sometimes, Irwin imagined they were his friends. He imagined that he was part of their group, just like he was tonight. It was easy to think that he'd been invited to the party and that as soon as he pushed away from the wall, he'd be engulfed in conversations and welcomed in groups.

But that was far from the truth. He didn't have friends or

anyone he was close to. Even the nice people avoided him because of his mother and her friends, and that would never change. Irwin was going to be alone all of his life, and he'd thought he'd finally accepted that a few years ago. Maybe he'd been wrong, because tonight, it hurt as much as it had when he'd first realized it.

He hated his life. He even hated his mother sometimes. She was his first bully, and the way she kept him away from everyone meant no one knew. They probably thought he was on her side and that he thought the same way she did.

Nothing could be further from the truth.

Irwin's stomach churned. He'd been excited at the thought of being here, even though he'd known he'd have to hide, but not anymore. He felt like he might be about to throw up, but he didn't want to do that in front of everyone. His place wasn't here. His place was in his room, hiding like he did most of the time.

He slid sideways, ready to leave, when movement caught his eye. He wasn't sure why it did. There were so many people here, all of them moving one way or another, so he shouldn't have noticed this one guy. For some reason, he did, and once he did, he couldn't look away.

Even from a distance, Irwin could see the guy was a Nix. He was moving toward a table at the back of the room, which meant that Irwin could see his pointed ear. His long blond hair was another clue, and Irwin was ready to bet that the man's eyes were green.

He wished he could get closer and check if he was right. He almost did, but then he remembered who he was and what would happen if anyone noticed him standing here. His mother would no doubt find out, and if she did, she'd make sure he paid for disobeying her orders.

So instead of pushing forward like he wanted to, Irwin moved back and through the doorway.

He could still hear the party as he walked away. He was pretty sure he'd be able to hear it even from his bedroom, and he wasn't sure how to feel about that. He wanted people to have fun, but it hurt not to be able to be part of it, and even more, not to be able to be part of this group of people. They were friends and family, something Irwin had never had and never would have.

Coming had been a mistake. He'd been doing well enough. He'd known he'd never have this kind of thing, and he'd accepted it.

Mostly. The fact that he'd decided to come, even knowing it would hurt, was probably a sign that he hadn't accepted his fate, no matter how hard he'd tried to convince himself that he had.

He wanted things to change but couldn't see a way to make it happen. His mother controlled him, and while he knew he could go to the alpha, so far, Gal hadn't done anything about her. She'd always been a bully, and he knew that was how she was. She was still here, though, which meant she wasn't going anywhere. That, in turn, meant that Irwin wasn't, either.

He was so distracted that he didn't see that his bedroom door was open until it was too late. He pushed it fully open and stepped into the room, freezing when he saw his mother sitting on his bed.

Her arms were crossed over her chest, and her back was ramrod straight. She glared at him, and that expression was enough for him to know he was about to regret everything he'd done tonight.

He quickly stepped back into the hallway but already knew his mother wouldn't let him go.

"Where do you think you're going?" she snapped as she followed.

The area of the house where he and his mother lived was empty right now. Everyone was at the party, so there wouldn't be anyone to hear what she was saying or to see what she'd do. Irwin knew that hiding and running from her would only delay the inevitable, so he stopped moving.

It wasn't easy to resist the urge to run. He always felt like that when she was angry because he knew she was about to hurt him. If he hid, though, she'd hurt him even more. It wouldn't be worth it.

He might as well face his punishment now.

He sucked in a breath and turned to face her. "Good evening," he whispered.

"Don't you *good evening* me," she answered. She was trying very hard to control her tone, but it didn't matter.

Irwin could read her better than he could read anyone else. He'd had to learn so he would make sure he wouldn't make her angry with his behavior.

Tonight, he had. Tonight, he'd allowed himself to hope and behave like a normal twenty-six-year-old man.

He shouldn't have.

He bowed his head. Saying anything right now would only make things worse. No matter how many questions his mother asked, she didn't actually expect him to answer. She already knew the answers, and she'd throw them in his face while expecting him to stay quiet and take everything.

He would. It was the only way for him to make it out of this without pain. It didn't always work, but his best bet was to go along with what his mother wanted, stay quiet and still, and allow her to scream.

When she slapped his shoulder, he winced. He'd been wrong. No matter what he did tonight, this *was* going to hurt.

It was just another normal day in his life.

"I'm going to find Miko," Thedric said.

He'd been rubbing Farley's back, trying to comfort him or

maybe to calm him down. Farley wasn't sure, and he didn't care. He was grateful for the contact, and even though he'd wanted to be alone so he could freak out seconds before, now he could feel himself panicking at the thought of Thedric leaving him.

"You don't have to go," he told him.

Thedric's eyes were wide, and he looked a little panicky. It was probably because he wasn't used to dealing with this kind of situation, but then, neither was Farley. What was happening? Why was he reacting this way?

He'd met his mate, so what? Miko had met his mate, too, and he hadn't freaked out like this. He'd taken time to get to know Robin, and now they were together and as happy as any other couple.

And Farley could have that, too.

He sucked in a breath, then another. "Did you react like this when you realized Les was your mate?" he asked Thedric.

"Are you asking if I panicked?"

"Yeah."

Thedric smiled. "I did. I was married, and my parents had all those expectations. I thought it would be a disaster."

"But it wasn't."

"Not at all. I'm the happiest I've ever been, and it's thanks to Les."

Farley nodded and straightened. "I'm fine."

"No offense, but you don't look fine. I know you said you didn't need Miko, but I'd feel better if you let me get him."

Farley huffed. "Fine. But don't tell him what happened."

"He'd want to know. He'll take one look at you and know something is going on."

"I need to tell him myself."

Thedric nodded, then stepped away and vanished into the crowd. Farley sucked in a breath, then another, and leaned against the wall.

What had he been thinking, hiding behind the table like that? He didn't have to go up to his mate as soon as he'd realized what they were to each other. He could have given himself time without hiding like an idiot.

He looked around, but he couldn't see his mate anywhere. He wasn't by that door anymore. The wall was empty, and no matter how hard Farley looked around the room for him, he couldn't see him.

"What happened?" Miko asked, suddenly appearing with Thedric by his side.

Farley didn't hesitate to throw himself into his best friend's arms. He pressed his forehead against Miko's shoulder, so relieved he felt he could cry. Even though he was still freaking out, he felt better after talking to Thedric, and Miko's presence was enough to calm him.

"I saw my mate," he explained.

Miko pushed him away but didn't let him go far. He grabbed his shoulders and kept him in place as they stared at each other. "Really?"

Farley nodded. "I wouldn't lie to you about something like that. He was right here."

"Who is he?"

"I don't know. The only people I know here are our friends and family. Most of the others are part of the pride."

"We need a pride member."

That would be best. They'd be able to tell Farley who his mate was and maybe even where he could find him. "Not Jordan. It's his birthday, and I don't want him to have to worry about me."

"I'll get Simon," Thedric said quickly before disappearing into the crowd again.

"This is a good thing," Miko said. "You don't have to bond with him immediately or even date him. You just have to get to know him."

"I don't know why I panicked."

"Because you didn't expect it." Miko beamed. "We always wondered what it would be like to be part of the pride, and now, you'll know."

Farley swallowed. He hadn't thought about that, but Miko was right. Unless his mate decided he didn't want to be a pride member anymore, Farley would become one, too. They'd have to talk to the alpha first, and the thought of the many things they'd have to explain and do made his head spin. He didn't know where to start.

Hopefully, his mate would.

"Hey," Simon said as he walked toward them. "Thedric said it was an emergency. What's going on?"

He looked worried, so Farley quickly reassured him as he stepped away from Miko. "I'm too dramatic, but I'm fine. I was just shocked because I saw my mate on the other side of the room and freaked out."

Simon grinned. "Really? Does that mean you're a pride member now?"

"I don't know. I have no idea who he is. I just saw him from afar. No matter how hard I try, I can't find him again, so he might have left."

"Why don't you describe him? I'll try to figure out who it is."

Farley closed his eyes. "From where he was, I think he's about as tall as me, maybe slightly shorter. He has brown hair that falls in front of his face, almost like he's using it to hide. I couldn't see the color of his eyes from where I was, but something in how he behaved made me worry. It was almost as if he was afraid someone would see him."

Which didn't make sense, because if he was a pride member, he had as much right to be there as any other pride member. Jordan hadn't invited a specific group of people except for his friends. The party was open to everyone in the pride, and since he was there, Farley's mate had to be a member.

He opened his eyes. He'd expected Simon to be confused or maybe sorry because he didn't know who Farley was talking about. Instead, he looked worried, which didn't bode well.

"What?" Farley asked—whatever Simon was worried about, he needed to know. His mate was involved, and that was all that mattered.

"I think I know who it is," Simon said, sounding cautious.

"Then tell me." Farley cleared his throat. "Please."

"There's one person whose description fits, including the hair and the fact that he looks afraid. His name is Irwin, and he's a pride member, like you thought."

"Where can I find him?"

"You need to know something before you look for him." Simon sucked in a breath. "I'm sure you heard that Val and I had trouble with a few people when we first met. Someone tried to make me think that he was cheating on me with them."

"I heard something about that." And he prayed the someone Simon was talking about wasn't his mate.

"Kevin was angry because we both applied to become Gal's assistant. He wanted me to drop it because he wanted the job, and he used whatever he could think of to push me to do it and to push me away from my mate."

Good. Simon had said that Farley's mate's name was Irwin, not Kevin. That meant Irwin hadn't been involved in this.

Hopefully.

"Kevin's best friend, Anne, supported him through all of it."

"The kitchen woman?"

"Yes. I see you've already heard of her."

"Jordan told me she wasn't happy about him not wanting

her food for the party."

"She wasn't, and everyone in the pride heard it. Well, Irwin is her son. She and Kevin are bullies. They're people you want to stay away from."

It was like a punch to the stomach. Surely, fate wouldn't have given Farley a bad person as a mate. He hadn't done anything to deserve that. "I need to talk to him. I'll be careful, but there's a reason he's my mate."

Simon nodded. "I wasn't trying to tell you to stay away from him. I need you to be cautious. As far as I know, Irwin has never participated in whatever his mother and Kevin have been up to. He's never done anything to me, anyway. That doesn't mean he's not like her, but even if he isn't, she's involved. She won't be happy about you being her son's mate. She'll make sure you know it, and if you continue to try to get to Irwin, she'll find a way to stop you."

Farley stood up straighter. "She can try, but I won't let her stop us from being together. If Irwin wants me, then he has me." And if Irwin's mother tried to hurt their relationship in any way, Farley wouldn't hesitate to go straight to the council.

Irwin's mother was still yelling. Every so often, she hit him on the shoulder or arm. He was relieved that she'd avoided his face so far. He was pretty sure it wouldn't last forever, but if he could get away with a slap or two, it would be better than he'd expected.

"I was extremely clear," she said. "I told you to stay away from the party. They didn't want me or my food, which means they didn't want you, either."

"I didn't stay long," Irwin whispered.

"I don't care how long you stayed. If anyone saw you, they'll tell the rest of the pride. Do you know what that's

going to be like for me? Everyone will know I have no authority over my son."

Irwin didn't say anything. He shouldn't have said anything earlier, either. His mother just needed to rant, and once
she was done, he'd be allowed to go to his room.

The problem was that she was riling herself up. She kept
pointing out what the others would think and how they
would feel about knowing that her son had been at the party,
and it made her angrier every time she mentioned it. Irwin
wanted to tell her she should stop thinking about it if it trou-
bled her so badly, but he knew better. So he stayed silent and
very still, waiting for the moment he'd be allowed to leave.

He retreated into his head like he usually did. It was the
easiest thing to do, and there, she couldn't hurt him with her
words. She could easily hurt him physically, though, which
she didn't hesitate to do.

This time, the slap was aimed at his face. His first instinct
was to step away or grab his mother's wrist, but he'd done
that a few times and had always regretted it. He'd pay for it
if he did anything to avoid his punishment, so he took it like
the good son he was.

"What the fuck?" a male voice asked. "What are you doing? Why are you hurting him?"

Irwin blinked and looked up. He expected a pride member
to have caught them. If that had been the case, his mother
would have probably been able to talk her way out of it. She'd
have said that Irwin had been rude or that he was trying to
hurt her first.

But it wasn't a pride member, or rather, not just. Simon was
there, looking pale and horrified. He was staring at Irwin with
a hand over his mouth, and the way he looked at him made
Irwin want to hide. He stepped toward his bedroom door, but
his mother caught his wrist and squeezed to the point of pain.
He wasn't able to keep in the squeak that came out of him,

and his mother gave him a good shake for it.

"Let him go!" the other man said.

It was the blond Nix Irwin had noticed earlier. What was he doing here, and why was he stopping Irwin's mother from punishing him?

"He's my son. I'll do whatever I want with him," Irwin's mother snapped.

"You can't *hurt* him. Do I have to go get your alpha? Because I will, and I assure you, he'll be interested in knowing what I saw."

Irwin's mother snarled, but she did let him go. He quickly rubbed the skin where she'd hurt him, trying to be as discreet as possible so she wouldn't notice him.

"Go to your room," she told Irwin. She turned toward Simon and the Nix. "I don't care what you tell the alpha. I had every right to do what I did."

She walked away, not once looking back. She knew Irwin would obey, and she was right.

He moved toward his bedroom door, but the Nix touched his arm before he could. Irwin cringed, even though there was no pain. He couldn't remember the last time anyone touched him like this, not to hurt him but to comfort him.

"Are you all right?" the Nix asked, moving closer.

"I'll leave the two of you alone," Simon said. "It's probably better if I go find Gal anyway."

"No," Irwin told him. "I'm fine. She didn't hurt me."

"Are you sure?" the Nix asked. "Because that looks like it's going to bruise," he added, gesturing at Irwin's wrist.

He gently took Irwin's hand and raised it. To do so, he had to move even closer, and that was when Irwin realized why the man had intervened.

He was Irwin's mate.

Irwin's eyes widened, and he quickly stepped back. He stared at the Nix, unable to comprehend what had just happened. He couldn't have a mate, especially not one who wasn't a tiger shifter and part of the pride. His mother would be furious and take it out on him. She'd think it was his fault and that he'd somehow chosen his mate, but that wasn't true. Shifters didn't choose their mates. No one did.

Irwin's mate raised his hands. "Sorry. I didn't mean to startle you. My name is Farley."

"You're my mate," Irwin blurted out.

"I am," Farley confirmed. "That's why I wanted to find you. I saw you earlier at the party, and I was so shocked that I didn't manage to get to you before you left. I asked Simon who you could be, and he recognized my description of you. He brought me here." Farley hesitated. "Do you want to talk about what happened with your mother?"

Irwin shook his head. "Nothing happened. I'm used to it."

"Irwin," Simon began.

But Irwin didn't want to hear what he had to say. He was terrified that Simon would tell him it was his fault and that he just needed to do what his mother demanded of him. The few times he'd tried talking to someone about what his mother did to him, that was what their answer had been. He didn't see why things should be different now.

"I'm fine. She didn't do anything she hasn't done before, so there's no need for you to step in." He turned to Farley. "I'm really sorry about this and the fact that you were saddled with me as a mate. You and I can't be together, and I hope you find someone else to love you. I'm sure you deserve it."

Farley frowned. "What are you talking about? I don't want anyone else. You're my mate."

This was too much for Irwin. He stumbled back into his room, slamming the door behind himself. He locked the door and quickly ran to the window. He could hear Farley knocking on his door and calling out for him, but he ignored it as he climbed onto the roof.

This was the only place where he could be alone. His mother had never found out that he spent time on the roof, and he hoped she never would.

It had been hard to stay away when Simon's mate and his friends had been working and repairing the roof, but now, it was all new and safe. Here, Irwin's mother wouldn't find him. Here, he could give himself time to accept the fact that he'd found his mate but could never have him.

Finding his mate should be the happiest moment in his life, but instead it made him want to cry, because he knew he couldn't have Farley. It wasn't fair, but Irwin's life had never been fair. He was also used to that, even though he hated it.

His mother controlled his life. No matter how many times he'd tried leaving her, he'd been brought back. The old alpha had made sure Irwin knew that if he disobeyed his mother, he'd be kicked out of the pride, and Irwin wasn't willing to risk it, even though they had a new alpha. He didn't know Gal well, but from what he'd heard from his mother and her friends, he wasn't a good person. That was probably all lies, but it was the only thing Irwin could count on.

He'd never be free, and he'd never be with his mate. He needed to accept that and move on. The problem was that he didn't know how to do that.

CHAPTER TWO

Farley's life had never been complicated. He had two loving parents, had lived in Green Hill his entire life, and had never had to worry about anything more than school and his friends. It had been a great way to grow up, and he loved his parents for giving him that.

Things were way more complicated now.

It wasn't just that Farley was still trying to figure out what he wanted to do in life. Now there was Irwin to add to the confusion, and Farley had no idea how to deal with him or what to do about the fact that they were mates.

His first instinct was to say that he didn't care who Irwin was or, better, who his mother was. Irwin's mother wasn't Farley's mate. She didn't have a say in their relationship and needed to stay away from it and leave Irwin alone.

But Farley knew how complicated families could be. He just had to look at Miko's to know for sure. His uncle had gotten married to a woman his parents had chosen for him, and while thankfully, she was a nice person and had let him go when he'd told her he'd met his mate, his parents had been another matter. Not only had they tried to force Thedric into staying with his wife, but they'd also attempted to get custody of Miko because they'd wanted to mold him into their heir. Luckily, Miko had already been eighteen and with his mate, so their plan had failed. Instead of getting him, they'd lost both their sons and their grandson.

Farley's problem was like a walk in the park compared to that. The problem in his relationship wasn't his. It was Irwin's, and it was clear that Irwin's mother was going to be a massive pain in the ass.

Farley wasn't looking forward to dealing with her.

That didn't mean he was giving up on Irwin. They were mates, and he wanted to give them a chance. They would never know if they could work together unless they tried, and he was looking forward to that. He was pretty sure Irwin was older than him, but not by much, and hopefully, he'd be okay with getting to know each other and waiting before bonding. Farley didn't want to rush into anything, especially because they didn't have a reason to.

Unless Irwin's mother gave them one.

He groaned and buried his face against his pillow. He needed to get up and help his mother around the house, but after last night, he couldn't stop obsessing over Irwin. He'd spent half the night trying to figure out a way to make things between them work. Even worse, he'd spent a lot of time thinking about how Irwin had been terrified of his mother. Seeing the way she'd hurt him had been enough for Farley to want to take him far away from her and never return him, but that wasn't his decision.

He rolled to his back and stared at the ceiling. He couldn't solve this for Irwin. Irwin had to want things to change, and while Farley hoped he did, he couldn't be sure until they talked. He supposed that would be next on his list. He needed to return to the pride house, find him, and make sure he was all right. Then they could talk about what came next for them, and even though Farley didn't want to, about Irwin's mother. He wanted to help Irwin, but he didn't know how or even if he could.

He grabbed his phone. Talking to Irwin would be the best thing to do, but he didn't know if Irwin would want to talk to him. The way he'd disappeared into his room last night and hadn't answered when Farley had knocked suggested that he might not want to see him today, which meant Farley would need to find his information through someone else. He could ask Simon, but he wasn't sure what Simon would do after what they'd both seen yesterday. He'd appeared as horrified as Farley had felt, and Farley couldn't help but wonder if Simon had known about this before. How was it possible that an adult man was being abused by his mother, and no one had noticed?

Farley didn't blame Simon if that was so. Even though the pride was small enough for all the members to live in the same house, it was clear there were different groups and factions, and apparently some of them stayed away from each other. If Irwin's mother was as horrible as Simon had said, it made sense for Simon not to want to spend any length of time with her.

But Simon wasn't the only pride member Farley knew. He hadn't wanted to say anything to Jordan yesterday because it was his birthday, but now it wasn't, and Farley was ready to poke him for answers.

He knew Nestor better than he did Jordan, so he called him. It was nine in the morning, and Jordan had a shift at the bookstore that morning, even though it was Sunday. He might be busy already, and Farley didn't want to bother him.

"Hello?" Nestor answered.

He sounded sleepy, but he didn't tell Farley to fuck off, which was a good sign.

"Hey. I was wondering if Jordan was still home or if he'd already gone to work."

"Why didn't you call him?"

"Because I didn't want to bother him if he was at work."

"He's here," Nestor said with a sigh.

There was some noise, and then Jordan came on the line. "Hey," he said. "Did something happen last night?"

"How do you know?"

"It's clear you don't know how prides are. When

something happens, the entire pride knows by the next day. I don't have any details, but I know you were involved."

"It's why I'm calling. I need your help."

"Depending on what it is, I can move my shift at the store."

"I don't want you to have to do that."

"I'll go," Nestor said in the distance. "It's been a while since I had a shift, and I kind of miss it. You and Farley go do whatever you need to do."

There were more sounds of Jordan and Nestor talking, and Farley gave them a moment. This was much more than he'd hoped for, and he felt kind of guilty about taking Jordan away from his job, especially because he didn't know if it was necessary. He just wanted answers for now, and Jordan could give him those on the phone.

"All right," Jordan said as he came back on the line. "Tell me what's going on."

Farley did. He'd called for help and answers, and Jordan needed to know everything to provide that. Farley told him about Irwin being his mate and about his encounter with Irwin's mother in the hallway. Even though he didn't want to betray Irwin's trust, he also told him what he'd seen her do to him. He didn't think Jordan knew anything about that, so he wasn't surprised when Jordan swore.

"I'd say I can't believe she did that, but I can," he said.

"Simon told me she wasn't a good person, but I didn't expect that."

"Saying she's not a good person would be an understatement. She's a resentful hag, and I hate that she's hurting her son. It explains a lot, though."

Farley's mouth went dry. "I expected it to. Can you tell me more about it?"

"I don't like feeling as if I'm betraying Irwin, but it's clear he needs help, and I don't think he'd ever ask for it. What are you going to do about him?"

"I don't know. I need more information before I try anything."

"You're not giving up on him?"

Jordan's tone gave Farley pause. Simon had asked that yesterday, too, and Farley had been convinced that he didn't want to give up. This was a second chance for him to think about it and possibly change his mind. Even though he wanted to say that he couldn't give up on his mate, he gave himself a moment to think about what being with Irwin would mean.

For one, Farley would have the most awful mother-in-law in the world. It wasn't something he knew how to deal with, but it was clear Irwin didn't, either, and he'd known her all his life. It wasn't fair to let him face all of this on his own, especially when Farley was his mate. Beyond that, Farley wasn't giving up on their relationship. He could tell it would take a lot of work, but that didn't scare him. He doubted Irwin could make any kind of promises when it came to their future, but then, neither could he. They just had to get to know each other and see what happened.

"I want to at least talk to him. I want to give our relationship a chance," he told Jordan.

Jordan sighed. "I was afraid you'd say that."

You can't stay locked in your room forever. I want to talk to you, and I want to do so now.

Irwin stared at the text on his phone. His mother had sent it early this morning, and he hadn't answered. He also hadn't answered the many phone calls, the other texts, or the knocks on his door.

She'd be pissed when he finally came out of his bedroom. He'd have to deal with the consequences of that when he couldn't stay any longer, but for now, he was safe. He might be hungry, but being a little hungry was something he was used to, and he wanted to be safe from his mother more than he wanted to eat.

Once, she'd had a key. She'd used it to come in and out of his bedroom even when he locked it, and he'd hated that. He needed a safe space from her, and while his bedroom wasn't exactly that, it was the only place where he could lock himself in. So he'd stolen the key she had, and even though she'd been pissed and had suspected he had it, he'd told her she'd probably lost it. She didn't have had another one, which meant that Irwin owned both of the keys to his bedroom and that she couldn't barge in now that he was locked in.

He relaxed on his bed, or at least, he tried to. His anxiousness was pushing him to go back to the roof and spend the day there, but it was raining, and even though his tiger wouldn't mind, it made the roof more dangerous. He didn't want to slip and fall, which meant he was stuck here and that he wasn't going anywhere. It gave him time to think, something he didn't usually enjoy. He already knew his life was messed up. It was even more messed up now that he'd found his mate.

He wasn't sure what it meant. He had no doubt that Farley was his mate, but did it change anything for him? It wasn't like Farley would come in to save him. He couldn't take Irwin away from his mother. No one could, and more importantly, no one even tried. After last night, Irwin wouldn't be surprised if Farley decided that he was too much bother. Who would want to deal with Irwin's mother?

Irwin cringed when he thought about what Farley and Simon had seen. He'd always been surprised that no one in the pride had seen his mother hurt him. The only people who had were her friends, and they'd never said anything. They used that knowledge to make fun of him for being beaten by a woman.

As far as Irwin knew, the rest of the pride didn't know. The old alpha knew, but Gal didn't. He would have already stepped in if he did, or at least Irwin hoped so. Things had never been great, but that had changed recently. Gal seemed to be a good alpha, but he couldn't be everywhere or solve problems he didn't know existed.

Irwin's stomach growled, but he ignored it. He also ignored his phone, even though it was vibrating on the bed.

He hated his life. He didn't know what he'd done to deserve a mother so horrible that she hurt her child, but it must have been bad. Had he been a murderer in a previous life? Was he paying for that now?

Irwin didn't know if he believed in that kind of thing, but it certainly felt like it was a possibility. He realized he wasn't the only one who had it bad in life, though. Hell, he was sure there were people who had it worse. His mother had terrorized him his entire life and regularly hit him, but that was it. She kept the bruises in places he could hide, and while it hurt, it was nothing he couldn't heal quickly from.

Still, a lot of the time, he wished he could climb out of the window and vanish. He wondered what his mother would do if he did. Would she be happy that she was finally rid of him, or would she freak out because she'd lost the one person she had complete control over? It was a hard question to answer.

The sound of a car approaching the house made him sit up. It was normal for pride members to go in and out of the house now, so he was getting used to the sound of cars, but he was always curious. Even after Gal had declared they were all free to find jobs and do whatever they wanted with their life, Irwin had never been allowed to leave this place. His mother had pitched a fit the only time he'd suggested it, and she'd kept an eagle eye on him ever since.

Maybe she'd miss him if he left. She wouldn't feel that way because she loved him or anything like that, though. She'd miss him because she wouldn't have control over him anymore. Irwin supposed *that* was what she'd miss the most.

He got up from his bed and peeked out the window. He expected it to be someone coming back from running an errand in town, but he recognized Jordan's car. That was odd, because Jordan didn't live at the house anymore. He'd come last night for his birthday party but didn't have a reason to be here this morning.

Irwin understood why he was there when he saw Farley in the passenger seat.

He swallowed. What was his mate doing here? Was he here to talk to him? That was the thing that made the most sense, but Irwin didn't know what to do. He wanted to talk to Farley, but at the same time, he didn't. He wanted to hide from him and not to have to explain what had happened last night. He was ashamed enough by what his mate had seen not to want to discuss it with him—or anyone else, for that matter.

Had Farley told Jordan? Was Jordan one more person who knew what Irwin's life was like?

Irwin's heart fluttered. He was starting to panic, and that was never a good thing. When he panicked, he didn't think. He acted on instinct, and with fear taking over, he did stupid things his mother punished him for later on.

Maybe he should stay in his bedroom. Here, he couldn't do anything stupid. He was safe, and no one could see him.

But Farley knew where Irwin's bedroom was. He'd been here last night, so he'd be able to find it easily enough. There was a chance he wasn't coming to Irwin's bedroom. Maybe he was going to see Gal and tell him that he and Irwin were mates.

That was even worse.

Irwin bit on his lower lip hard so he wouldn't freak out. He was more than halfway there but needed to keep his cool.

He had no idea how to do that. He'd never been able to before and didn't know where to start. Maybe he didn't *have* to keep his cool. Maybe he could just shut down like he did when his mother raged against him and hit him. He could get through this the same way, and hopefully, by the time he was calmer, Farley would have left.

Irwin watched his mate climb out of Jordan's car. Even at a distance, he was beautiful, and Irwin yearned for him. He wanted to get to know him. He wanted to find out what Farley liked and what he disliked, what he looked like first thing in the morning, and maybe even at night, when the world outside was sleeping. He wanted a relationship with his mate, a future.

He couldn't see a way to have any of that.

Irwin was a prisoner in his own life and his bedroom. No matter how much he wanted Farley to be his knight in shining armor, he wasn't. He was just a man who had no clue what he was walking into.

"I could have shimmered us here," Farley said again.

Jordan rolled his eyes. "It's fine. I like to drive."

"I'm sorry I pulled you away from your job."

Jordan came to stand in front of him. "I wouldn't be here if I didn't want to. My brother-in-law knows that I needed to be with you today, and besides, it's not like I left him in trouble. Nestor was happy to work my shift. I'll go there once we're done, so please, stop worrying and focus on the reason we're here today."

Farley turned to look up at the house. He was pretty sure that Irwin's bedroom was on this side of the house, and he wondered which window belonged to him. He couldn't remember well from last night, but maybe if he looked up, he'd be able to see his mate hiding behind one of them.

"So what's the plan?" Jordan asked.

Farley snorted. "You thought I had a plan?"

"I hoped it would be better than talking to Irwin and seeing what happened, but let's do that."

"So you think I should go to Irwin's bedroom and talk to him?"

Farley wasn't even sure Irwin would want to talk to him. He'd been terrified yesterday when Farley had tried, and he'd refused to open the door or to talk to Farley through it. Once he'd locked himself in, there hadn't been a sound, and Farley had been scared something had happened to him. Simon had tried to reassure him, but worry still gnawed at his heart.

He looked up again, and this time, he saw something move behind one of the windows. He squinted, and while he couldn't see well, he was pretty sure it was his mate. If the way the silhouette disappeared as quickly as it had appeared was anything to go by, Irwin didn't want to talk to Farley this morning, either.

"I think we should talk to Gal," Jordan said.

"The alpha?"

Jordan nodded. "He needs to know what's happening. He's had a lot of work to do and things to deal with since he became alpha, so I'm not surprised he missed this, but he'll be angry that he has. He won't want Irwin to continue being hurt by his mother. He already dealt with her before. He knows what kind of person she is, so he won't be surprised to hear what you have to say."

"I don't know if going behind Irwin's back to your alpha will help." If the alpha didn't know, there had to be a reason.

Unless Irwin's mother stayed with him the entire day, he'd had the opportunity to go to the alpha or the beta anytime he wanted. Why hadn't he talked to them already? Why was he allowing his mother to hurt him?

Farley knew nothing about abuse and how the people being hurt reacted. He didn't want to judge, and he knew better than to think he had all the answers. He didn't even have any of them. Whatever was going on in Irwin's life, it couldn't be easy for him to go up to a man he barely knew and tell him that his mother abused him.

"All right. Let's go to your alpha," he agreed.

Jordan looked both relieved and worried at the same time. That didn't bode well, but nothing in this situation did.

The only thing Farley wanted was to get Irwin away from this place. It wasn't good for him, and he wasn't sure it ever would be. Even if Irwin's mother was dealt with, there had to be many bad memories between these walls. How could Irwin stand to live here? Would he want to stay once this was over?

Was Farley making a mistake?

This could turn into a disaster in which Farley would lose his mate, and he wasn't ready to face that. He tried not to think about that. He'd deal with it if it happened. Until then, he'd convince himself that everything was peachy.

Things went sideways almost as soon as Farley stepped into the house. A man was walking by, eating a cookie as he looked down at his phone. When he heard the front door, he looked up, his eyes narrowing at the sight of Jordan, then even more so when he saw Farley.

"He's not a pride member," he said.

Jordan tensed, which was enough to tell Farley this was going to be a problem. He wanted to help but had no idea who this guy was or what he should do or say, so he kept his mouth shut and let Jordan handle it.

"I'm aware of that," Jordan said.

"Then what is he doing here?"

"He's my friend, Kevin. He was here yesterday, too."

Kevin wrinkled his nose. "During your little birthday party? Half the town was here, and it was horrible. This is a pride house. Only pride members should be allowed in. I don't want him here, and I don't think anyone else does, either. He needs to leave."

Jordan breathed in and out as if he was trying to keep himself calm. "You don't make the rules, and you don't give me or anyone else orders," he said slowly. "Gal has already declared it was okay for people to have visitors, which is what Farley is. He's not staying. He's just visiting, and he'll leave once he's done."

Kevin wasn't giving up. "What are you doing here, anyway? You don't live here anymore. This isn't your home."

"I might not live here, but I'm still a pride member."

"Well, maybe you shouldn't be. Every pride member lives here. Why should you have special rules?"

Farley hadn't realized he already knew who Kevin was, or rather, that he'd been told about him. Listening to his words made him remember. Simon had said that Kevin had kissed his mate to try to make them break up. He'd been angry at Simon for applying for the assistant job and got his revenge by kissing Val.

Farley was tempted to tell Kevin to fuck off just for that. The fact that he was standing between Farley and his mate wasn't helping, either. All in all, Kevin sounded like a horrible person Farley didn't want anything to do with. For some reason, he seemed to have decided to appoint himself guardian of the pride or something like that, and Farley could tell it wouldn't be easy to get past him.

Then the situation turned worse. A door by the stairs opened, and Irwin's mother stepped through. Her gaze zeroed in on Farley as if she'd known he was there, and while Kevin had been pissed at Farley's presence, it was clear she was *furious*.

"What are you doing here?" she demanded to know. "How dare you come into my house after what you did last night?"

Farley had no idea how to deal with these two. He didn't want to create trouble or to make a scene, even though he wasn't the one doing so. They were doing it all by themselves, and it was a miracle no one had heard them yet.

Maybe someone had but had decided they didn't want to be involved. Farley could understand that. He didn't want to be involved in any of this, either. Unfortunately, there was no way for him not to be. If he wanted to be there for his mate, he needed to see him, and eventually, he'd have to face his mother.

Facing a dragon sounded easier.

"You're not the alpha," Jordan pointed out.

Irwin's mother looked even angrier. "I don't need to be. I've lived here since before you were born, boy. I might not be the alpha, but I have authority and don't want either of you here. You don't belong with us anymore. You decided you didn't want to be a pride member, and this is the consequence. I don't care what the alpha says. This is my home more than it can ever be his, and you need to leave."

Farley hadn't known what would happen today, but he wished he could go back in time and do this differently, even though he doubted her reaction would have been any different.

Irwin could hear the shouting from his bedroom. He recognized the voice from having heard it screaming at him at least once a day since he was born, and he cringed at the thought that his mother had found out that Farley was here. She didn't know he was Irwin's mate, but he was making it clear that he was interested in Irwin, which meant Irwin would be in trouble as soon as Farley left.

And he *would* leave. Who would want to stay when they were being yelled at for nothing more than being in a home where they didn't live? Irwin's mother was shouting so loudly that Irwin could hear her every word, so he knew what she was saying.

He was angry. Jordan would always be a pride member. The fact that he lived in town didn't change that. Unless he decided to join another pride, this was his home. It was the house where he'd been born and where he'd lived until he'd moved out. He had as much right to be here as Irwin's mother, no matter what she was yelling.

Farley, on the other hand, wasn't a tiger shifter. He wasn't a pride member. He hadn't grown up here, and Irwin doubted he'd ever move in. That didn't mean he wasn't allowed to be here. Irwin couldn't hear what Jordan was saying because he wasn't shouting, but he had no doubt that was what he was explaining. Farley was his friend, and every pride member was allowed visitors.

Irwin swallowed. He wanted to go downstairs and see what was happening. He wanted to tell Farley that he wasn't worth the hassle and that he should leave. The less he interacted with Irwin's mother, the better it would be for him. He didn't need her kind of person in his life and in his future, but if he insisted on trying to get to Irwin, he'd *have* to deal with her.

Irwin's stomach churned at the thought of his mother finding out he and Farley were mates. He had seen her angry many times over the years, but that would make all those times look like fun. She'd explode and take every bit of anger and resentment out on him. She'd blame him for it, even though fate made the decisions when it came to mates.

Irwin couldn't have chosen better for himself. Farley was beautiful, and even though they hadn't spoken much, he seemed gentle and caring. Anyone else would have stayed away after last night, but he'd come back. Irwin was sure he was here for him, to try to talk to him again. Knowing that touched something in him, and while it was almost as scary as having to deal with his mother, Irwin forced himself to face that emotion.

If he and Farley could make it work, he wouldn't be alone anymore. He wasn't sure it was a good thing to pull Farley into this mess, but after all, Irwin wasn't the one doing so. Fate had decided that Farley needed to be by Irwin's side, and maybe there was a reason it was happening now. Maybe Farley had been sent to help Irwin.

Irwin swallowed. He couldn't put that kind of responsibility on his mate's shoulders. If he wanted out of the pride house and his mother's claws, he should be the one working toward that. He shouldn't need someone to protect him and shield him from her anger. He should be strong enough to stand up to her.

The problem was that he didn't think he was.

He hated all of this. He hated the control his mother had over him, as well as every time she'd hurt him and every time she would try to hurt him in the future. He didn't want to have to deal with her ever again. He didn't want her to be his mother, even though there was no way out of that.

He wanted to get out of this house and to go as far as possible and never come back.

He looked out the window. He would climb on the roof, even though it was raining, but that would only give him a few moments of respite. Considering what was happening downstairs, his mother would be back at his door soon. She wouldn't let it go this time. She'd pound until he opened, and if he didn't, she'd find another way inside. He'd have to deal with her, even though there was nothing he wanted less. The only way to avoid it would be to leave.

Irwin didn't have a car. He couldn't drive because his mother had never allowed him to take lessons, saying it would be too dangerous and that he would be unable to learn. Maybe she truly thought he was an idiot, or maybe she was trying to convince him that he was. Maybe she was right, and he would never be able to learn. It looked complicated and scary.

But he didn't need to drive to leave the house. He didn't even need to walk.

He scrambled to open the window, ignoring the light rain. He was careful because everything was slick, but he was used to climbing in and out of his window. This time, instead of going up, he went down.

It was more complicated. Once he was out of the window, he decided it would be better for him to do this in his tiger form. He'd be heavier but also more agile and could jump the rest of the way down. He wouldn't hurt himself, but he'd end up naked in the trunk of Jordan's car.

He bit on his lower lip. That wouldn't be the best way to make this work. Once the car stopped, he'd have to sneak out and find a place to stay in town. Maybe he could stay in his tiger form and sleep in a park.

That would be a problem for later. For now, he quickly undressed and dropped his clothes into his room. He kept his phone in a case with a lanyard, so he hooked it around his neck, shifted, then jumped. In his form tiger, it was nothing.

He had to shift back when he reached the car to open the trunk, but once he was inside, he shifted back. He closed it and prayed he wouldn't suffocate. He hadn't completely thought this through, but it was too late to stop. He was locked in the trunk now.

He wasn't sure how long it took, but eventually, he heard the front door open and close. Two sets of footsteps came closer, and he held his breath as he listened.

"I'm sorry you didn't manage to talk to Gal," Jordan said.

"It's fine. I can always come back, and it was better to leave, considering what was happening."

"I fucking hate them."

"I don't know them, but I can't say I like them much."

They climbed into the car. It moved under Irwin's body, and he held his breath, hoping they wouldn't notice he was hiding back there. When the engine turned on, he allowed himself to relax. The car moved, and the further it got away from the house, the more excited Irwin became. He wiggled a bit, unable to stay still.

He'd never been this far away from the pride house. His mother had never allowed him to leave. He'd never even been in town, and while the thought of what he'd see there was frightening, the freedom he now had was a feeling so big he couldn't wrap his mind around it.

He was free.

That was, he was until the car stopped.

The doors opened again, and he waited to see what would happen. Jordan was probably dropping off Farley. Irwin wished he could see where Farley lived.

The trunk opened.

Irwin sucked in a breath and tried to curl himself into a tight ball, but he was a tiger. There was no way for him to make himself small.

"I told you I'd heard something," Jordan said.

Both he and Farley were looking down at Irwin.

"Who is it?" Farley asked.

"No idea, but I can take a guess."

Farley stared at Irwin. Irwin had no idea what he was thinking or how he felt, but he was scared.

"Irwin, if that's you, you can come out. You can spend the rest of the day and the night at my house," Farley said softly. "You don't have to say anything, and we don't have to talk about what happened last night or the fact that we're mates. It's clear you need time, and I want to give that to you. I also want to give you a safe place." He paused and cocked his head. "But if you're not Irwin, get the fuck away from me."

It looked like Irwin had found where he'd be going next.

Chapter Three

Farley hadn't thought he'd be able to sleep with Irwin next to him, but he'd been wrong. He'd slept like the dead, even after everything that had happened over the past two days. Having Irwin next to him made him feel at peace, even though there were so many things they needed to talk about and so many decisions to make.

Yesterday, it had been clear that Irwin was overwhelmed, so Farley hadn't pushed. After he and Jordan had found the tiger shifter in the trunk of Jordan's car, he hadn't wanted to overwhelm him. Irwin had probably heard his mother shouting and had decided to sneak out. Farley didn't know if he'd done so to be with him or just because he wanted out of the house, but when he'd offered for Irwin to spend the day and night at his place, Irwin had promptly agreed.

It was a good thing the tiger *was* Irwin.

Farley still wasn't entirely sure why Irwin had decided to shift to run away, but the result was that when he shifted back, he'd been naked. Thankfully, Jordan kept spare clothes in his trunk, probably because he was used to this kind of situation. Farley wasn't a shifter, so he'd never needed a change of clothes in his car. Of course, he also didn't have a car, because he shimmered anywhere he needed to go.

But it was good that Jordan had been able to give Irwin some clothes. It would have been odd to introduce Irwin to Farley's parents while he was naked. They would have understood when Farley explained he was a tiger shifter, but still. He hadn't yet told them that Irwin was his mate, and he

36

wasn't sure when to do it.

He turned onto his side and peeked at Irwin. It wasn't the first time Farley had a sleepover, although usually it was Miko sleeping next to him in the bed. His parents had never had any problem with it, even though Farley was gay. They'd known Miko was his best friend and that there was nothing beyond that between them. They'd been slightly more hesitant when Farley asked if Irwin could stay because they didn't know him, but his mother had declared that Farley was nineteen, and as long as they kept the noise down, she wouldn't order her adult son around.

Farley had great parents and was ever so thankful for that after meeting Irwin's mother.

He wanted to reach out and touch Irwin's cheek but didn't want to wake him up. He suspected that Irwin didn't often have the opportunity to sleep as much as he was. He wouldn't be surprised if Irwin's mother forced him to get up early every morning just because she could. She clearly enjoyed her control over him, and Farley couldn't help but wonder if Irwin could ever get out from under her thumb. They barely knew each other, so he had hope but wasn't sure where to go from here.

The first thing would be to be honest, both with Irwin and with his parents. Even though Farley wanted nothing more than to stay here and stare at Irwin until he woke up, he and his parents needed to talk. Considering the kind of woman Irwin's mother was, there was no way to know what her reaction would be at the news that Farley was her son's mate, and Farley wanted the people he cared about to be ready for whatever she threw at them. He hated that he was being rushed into this, but he had to deal with what fate had given him, and he would.

After watching Irwin for a moment longer, Farley got up. He used the bathroom and then headed downstairs. He could smell breakfast in the air, and while it made his stomach grumble, he wasn't sure he'd be able to eat before telling his parents about Irwin. They'd know something was wrong right away if he didn't eat, though.

"Good morning," he told them as he walked into the kitchen.

His father looked up from the pan on the stove and smiled, while his mother gestured for him to sit next to her.

"Is your friend still sleeping?" she asked, leaning forward.

She was eager to talk about Irwin. Maybe it would make Farley's job easier.

Or maybe it would make it harder.

He cleared his throat. "Yeah. He doesn't often have the opportunity to sleep late."

Farley's mother nodded. "I guessed something like that. Are you going to tell us about him?"

"The situation is complicated."

"Is it his parents? He looked so surprised at some of the things your father and I did, and I didn't understand why he'd react that way until I realized he probably didn't have this at home. He's an adult, right?"

"Yeah, but he's a tiger shifter, so he lives with the pride."

"I see. Was it really bad before the alpha changed? Is that why your friend is like this?"

"I don't know how much I can tell you because I haven't talked to him yet, but things are pretty bad with his mother, and he doesn't have his father anymore." Jordan had mentioned something about Irwin's father dying when he was a child, and while Farley hadn't dared to ask Irwin, Jordan didn't have a reason to lie to him.

"We'll do whatever we can to help," Farley's father said as he brought breakfast to the table. "I filled a plate for Irwin and put it in the oven for when he's ready to eat."

Farley could cry. His parents didn't have to take Irwin in.

They didn't know he was Farley's mate yet, so they could have just as easily told him that Irwin needed to leave. Instead, they were already caring for him as if he were their son.

Farley wasn't afraid of their reaction about Irwin being his mate, but that didn't mean he was looking forward to telling them. He already knew that while they'd be happy for him, they'd also be hesitant because he was so young. They could see that Miko and Robin were making it work, but even though they loved Miko like a son, he wasn't *their* son. Farley was, so this would touch closer to home.

"I wanted to thank you for welcoming Irwin the way you did," Farley said as he looked down at his plate of eggs and bacon. "He's not used to this kind of behavior from anyone, and he needed it. He's probably going to need it many more times in the future."

"He's always welcome here," Farley's mother promised.

"Well, I'm glad to hear that, because he's my mate."

The words were out, and Farley was already wondering if he'd done it the right way. Should he have waited longer? Should he have said it differently or given his parents time to wrap their minds around what he'd explained about Irwin? He had no idea, but it was too late. The truth was out.

For a moment, the kitchen was silent. It was as if a bomb had exploded, and Farley could have sworn his ears were ringing. He wanted to beg his parents to please say something but didn't want to rush them, so he pressed his lips together instead. He had to give them time.

His father was the first to react. He opened his mouth, closed it, then opened it again. "I'm not going to ask if you're sure because you wouldn't have told us if you weren't," he said slowly.

"I'm more than sure. It only took one look."

"Of course it did. How do you feel about it? Are you happy with the mate fate gave you?"

Once again, Farley's parents were only thinking about his happiness. His eyes burned, but he didn't want to cry, not even from happiness. He was pretty sure they'd freak out and think they'd done something wrong.

"Well, I don't know him well. I first saw him two days ago at Jordan's birthday party, and when I went to see him yesterday, things didn't go the way I expected. Like I said before, his situation is complicated, and it's not going to be easy for either of us to find a way to make it work."

"You're both so young," Farley's mother said. She reached for his hand and squeezed it. "You're only nineteen. I'm not saying it can't work, but you're really going to have to think about things before you act. I know you see Miko and Robin happy, and I want the same for you, but you need to be careful, especially if Irwin's situation is as complicated as you say it is."

"We're not rushing into anything, I promise. I feel I'm too young for this, too, and I'm not planning on bonding with him anytime soon." He didn't think Irwin would want it so soon, anyway. It would feel too much like control, and Irwin had enough of that with his mother.

His mother nodded. "Good. I want you to know that whatever decision you and Irwin make, you can always come to me or your father. We'll be here for you and Irwin, whatever happens. You're an adult, and we're not going to try to interfere in your relationship with Irwin, but it doesn't mean you can't count on us." She smiled. "I'm happy you found the person you'll spend the rest of your life with. It's a wonderful feeling, isn't it?"

Even with all the complications and not knowing what was going to happen or how to deal with Irwin's mother, she was right.

It *was* a wonderful feeling.

When Irwin woke up, he didn't have to wonder where he was, even though he wasn't in his bedroom. His mate's scent was all around him, telling him he was safe.

He opened his eyes to stare at the unfamiliar ceiling, almost afraid to look to the side. He'd been surprised when Farley had declared they'd have to share a bed, and he'd thought Farley was saying it because he wanted something to happen between them. He'd panicked because he'd never done that with anyone. Hell, he'd never even kissed anyone. He'd tried, but somehow, his mother had always found out when he had a crush on someone. She'd been a terror even when he was younger and made sure no one wanted to come anywhere near Irwin. There had only been a handful of guys Irwin's age in the pride and even fewer in whom he was interested, but after the one time she'd thrown a tantrum when she'd found Irwin with one of them, everyone had stayed away.

But not Farley. He'd already been yelled at twice, yet he seemed to want to spend time with Irwin anyway. Irwin might have expected him to want something more, but even after they'd gone to bed, Farley had kept to his side. He hadn't reached for Irwin, hadn't demanded Irwin do anything. He'd said good night and had fallen asleep, leaving Irwin to stare at him, unable to believe what was happening.

Irwin knew that his mate was supposed to be perfect for him and all of that. It was what all the stories said and what he'd seen in the couples around the pride. They seemed to be perfect for each other, and he'd always dreamed that he'd eventually find someone like that, too.

And he had. Farley was perfect, and while Irwin was terrified, he also couldn't wait to see what would happen between them.

But he had to remind himself that this was temporary. He hadn't moved in with Farley and his parents. He hadn't moved out of the pride house. He'd run away.

He winced when his gaze found his cell phone on the nightstand. That was the only thing he'd brought along, but he'd turned it off and was afraid to turn it back on. Even though he always spent as much time as he could in his bedroom, his mother had to have realized he'd run away by now, and she'd be pissed.

Going back was going to be horrible. Irwin had seen other families in the pride, so he'd always known that the way his mother treated him wasn't the norm. Yesterday, as he watched Farley with his parents, it had been even more obvious. They loved him and wanted him to be happy. At dinner, they'd talked about what Farley could do next since he'd graduated high school. Farley had admitted that he didn't know yet, and they'd told him that they weren't in a rush for him to find his path. He was looking for a job so he could contribute, but it had been clear that he'd always be welcome in this house. His parents wouldn't kick him out. They loved him, and he loved them.

Irwin tried to remember his father. Had he been like Farley's father? Had he loved him and treated him right? And what about his mother? Had she always been like this, or had things changed when his father had died? Irwin's parents hadn't been mates. Back then, with the old alpha, pride members weren't allowed to leave pride territory. They couldn't go out there and try to find their mates or even just happiness. Their place had been with the pride, and if they wanted a relationship, they had to choose someone who was already a pride member.

That was what Irwin's parents had done. They'd decided they liked each other well enough and had Irwin. They'd never been married or anything like that. No one got married at the pride. They'd just been together until Irwin's father died.

What was Irwin going to do? He had to go back, but he knew what a catastrophe that would be. His mother was going to make sure he never saw the light of day again. She'd want revenge, and the thought was scary enough to make Irwin wonder if he could stay here. He could hide in Farley's closet and stay out of the way, and Farley's parents wouldn't even notice him.

He'd been tempted to beg to stay last night at dinner, but he'd managed to keep his mouth shut. He had no idea if Farley was ever going to tell them he and Irwin were mates, but even though Irwin knew he probably wouldn't, he couldn't help but hope.

It wasn't right for fate to saddle Farley with a mate like Irwin, but there was no getting out of it. Neither of them had a choice, so they had to deal with what fate had handed them. In Farley's case, it was the mess that Irwin and his life were. He'd definitely gotten the short straw, and Irwin didn't know how to help him. If he could fix his life, he would, but he couldn't see a way out from his mother's claws. He was even afraid to allow himself to think about what a life without her would be.

The sound of footsteps made him jump. He scrambled toward the headboard, grabbing a pillow and hugging it to his chest. It smelled of Farley, which helped calm Irwin's racing heart, but then the door opened, and Irwin considered jumping out of the window.

"Good morning," Farley said as he walked in and saw that Irwin was awake.

Irwin told himself to calm down, but he didn't know if he could. Was Farley here to tell him he needed to leave? It would make sense. Farley had been a good person and a good mate yesterday when he'd allowed Irwin to stick around. He'd even let him stay the night, share his bed, and have dinner with him and his family. It was too much already, so Irwin wasn't surprised it was over.

"I'll go," he said in a strangled voice.

He started sliding to the side of the bed, but Farley raised a hand.

"What are you talking about?"

"I realize I've been here too long. I'll go before your parents can ask more questions."

They'd had a lot of those yesterday, and even though Farley had reassured him that they'd just been curious and wanted to get to know him better, Irwin wasn't sure about that. They had to wonder who he was and why Farley had dragged him here to spend the night. Irwin didn't think Farley would want them to know they were mates, so he hadn't said anything. That hadn't been easy, because every fiber of his being wanted to claim Farley.

"I don't want you to leave." Farley's eyes widened. "Well, I realize you'll have to go home eventually, but you don't have to rush out. Why don't you come downstairs to have breakfast? My parents want to say hello before they go to work."

The panic was still there, firmly wedged in Irwin's chest. "It's all right. I don't want to be more of a bother than I've already been. I can never thank you enough for what you did for me. You and your parents are incredible, and you gave me a day and night where I didn't have to worry about my mother."

Irwin snapped his mouth shut. Farley already knew what a disaster his life and his relationship with his mother were, and Irwin didn't need to give him any more details. Farley wouldn't want to hear that this was the first time he'd slept away from the pride house or how it had been years since he'd eaten dinner with anyone. His mother had forbidden him to eat with the rest of the pride long ago, and he'd always obeyed. At least she didn't force him to eat with her.

Even though he was stuck in that house with her, the less he saw her, the happier he felt.

Farley had no idea what had made Irwin panic. Was it something he'd said or done? It was almost as if Irwin had expected him to kick him out as soon as he woke up, and he didn't like that Irwin thought that way about him.

Irwin didn't know him. Right now, he was letting his doubts and fears take over, and he was panicking. Farley wanted to help him through it, and while he wasn't sure how, he'd find a way. There was a reason he was Irwin's mate, and he suspected that part of it was that he needed to keep Irwin safe, both from his mother and himself.

"You haven't been a bother," he said as he moved forward.

He didn't want to spook his mate, so he was careful when he sat on the edge of the bed. Irwin was still pressed against the headboard, hugging Farley's pillow as if it was a lifeline.

"Your parents had to cook for one more person, and you had to share your bed with me. How is that not a bother?"

"I wouldn't have invited you to spend the day with me and the night here if I hadn't wanted you to. My parents didn't have to cook. They could have ordered takeout, which would have been fine, but they enjoy cooking, especially for others. When it's just the three of us, it's not as fun, or at least, that's what they say."

Irwin shook his head. "It doesn't make sense. They don't know me, and I'm sure they want their home back, so I should go."

"Irwin, I'm not saying they want you to move in, but you're my mate. They're not going to kick you out just because you ate dinner with us and overslept this morning."

Irwin's eyes went wide. "You told them I'm your mate?"

Maybe Farley should have talked to him before doing so,

but he hadn't wanted to lie to his parents. It had been uncomfortable enough yesterday. "Yeah, I told them this morning while you were sleeping. I felt it was the right thing to do."

"You did what you felt was best for you and your family."

"And for you. I don't want to hide the fact that you're my mate. I don't want to hide it from my parents and friends. It won't change the way they behave with you, so you don't have to worry. You were welcome in our home yesterday and are still welcome now."

"I'm sure they wanted someone better for you," Irwin whispered.

"They don't know you. They believe in fate, though. You're my mate, which means there's no one better for me."

"That's not possible. You've met my mother. She's made my life hell since I was a child, and she hasn't stopped. Instead of standing up to her, I go along with it. I'm not brave. If anything, I'm a coward, and you deserve someone better. I feel fate has made a mistake, and it's not fair to you."

Farley wasn't sure which was worse, the panic or the self-deprecation. It was clear Irwin didn't see himself the way Farley did. As far as Irwin was concerned, he was nothing. He wasn't important to anyone, and he wasn't strong. He probably thought he didn't deserve to have a mate at all, which couldn't be further from the truth.

Under all of that fear and other complicated emotions was a man Farley wanted to get to know. He suspected Irwin didn't know himself, though. How could he, when he'd never been given the opportunity to be his own person? From what he was saying and what Farley had seen, Irwin's mother had controlled him his entire life. She'd never allowed him to find something he wanted to do for a living or to have friends or relationships. He'd been shielded from life in the worst way, and he was lost.

That wasn't his fault. It was his mother's fault, and Farley had to remind himself that he shouldn't yell at her when he saw her again. She'd hurt his mate, but that was over now, or at least, Farley hoped so. That would depend on Irwin, and Farley wasn't sure how his mate would take all of this. Farley wouldn't allow anyone to hurt Irwin, not even Irwin's mother.

She didn't deserve Irwin. Anyone else in Irwin's place would have been bitter. Maybe they would have become like her. Farley couldn't imagine Irwin as a bully but was surprised his mate hadn't gone down that path. It would have been the easiest way to get his mother off his back and get some control back. Instead, he'd curled in on himself and kept away from everyone else because he didn't want to hurt them.

Farley licked his lips. He needed to find a way to be honest with Irwin without freaking him out even more than he already was.

He turned to face him. Irwin's eyes were wide, and he was still clutching the pillow. He'd showered last night, and Farley had given him some of his clothes. They were too big on him, but Farley loved seeing it. It felt almost like Irwin was carrying a piece of Farley, and it felt right because they were mates.

"You and I are mates. Nothing can change that, and I don't want it to change," he said. "But I realize it doesn't mean that everything is all right in your world. We need to talk, and the conversation has to be a serious one about what's next for us. I need you to do something for me, though."

Irwin blinked. "Anything."

"Don't make that promise when you don't know what I'm about to ask."

"You wouldn't hurt me."

The absolute conviction in Irwin's voice made Farley want to weep. He didn't understand how his mate could be so trusting after everything his mother had put him through, but he promised himself that he wouldn't betray that trust. He'd never hurt Irwin on purpose. He would never forgive himself if he did.

"When we talk, I need you to believe me," Farley said. "I understand that you feel like I can't want you and like fate made a mistake, but I don't. I'm confused and realize it's complicated, but I know how I feel, and I need you to believe me. I won't lie to you. I won't tell you what I think you want to hear if it's not something I want. I think as long as we promise to be honest with each other, we can work this out." And hopefully, be happy together.

"I'm always going to have doubts," Irwin whispered, looking down at the pillow.

"And that's all right. I'm not asking you to change the way you feel. I understand this is going to be complicated and take time, but we can't work anything out if you don't give me a chance, and I feel you can't when you don't believe what I say. I get that you don't know me and that I could be lying to you even when I'm saying that I never will, but I feel like the only way to make this work is to trust each other."

Irwin didn't answer right away. Farley gave him time because, unlike Irwin's mother, Farley didn't want him to do something he wasn't ready for.

"I'll do my best," Irwin said eventually. "I'll try hard not to listen to the voice in the back of my mind that says that you're lying because you want to get rid of me."

Farley snorted. "There's nothing easy about you or our situation, but I don't want to get rid of you. I want to see where this goes. I want to make you happy."

"I want to make you happy, too."

Farley got up. "Good. Then we'll talk after breakfast. Are you ready to see my parents again?"

"Do I really have to? They know I'm your mate now."

"And they're excited to talk to you."

"I don't think anyone has ever been excited to talk to me."

"I was after I first saw you at Jordan's party."

Irwin stared for a moment, but something in his eyes told Farley that he believed him. It was a tiny step forward, but it *was* a step forward, which was more than Farley had hoped for.

Irwin was confused. He wanted to believe his mate, but he wasn't sure he should. Farley was saying all the right things, but Irwin had been hurt by someone who should have cared about him. His mother hadn't been able to love him, so who was to say that Farley would?

Irwin had no way of knowing what would happen with Farley. He could only trust what Farley said, and even though he wasn't sure he should, he wanted to.

Irwin had to remember that Farley wasn't his mother. That didn't mean he was a good person or that he wasn't lying, but it was enough for Irwin to want to give him a chance. Their bond had something to do with that, but the thought of what he'd lose if he didn't allow Farley in was too painful even to consider it.

He wanted to give Farley a chance because he was offering him a future that he'd never thought he'd have. It wasn't just for a way out from his mother.

He was only twenty-six, yet he'd already given up on having anything he could want in his life. He'd always thought he'd never have a job or relationship, that he'd have to live with his mother ordering him around for the rest of his life, or at least, for the rest of hers. He'd accepted his fate a while ago, but maybe he shouldn't have.

He wasn't alone anymore, and while it was confusing, it also gave him hope.

That didn't mean that dealing with all of this was easy. As

he followed Farley out of the bedroom, knowing he couldn't hide in there forever, he had to resist the urge to bolt. Farley's parents had been nice to him yesterday, and hopefully that wouldn't change from finding out that he was Farley's mate.

Breakfast with them was Irwin's first worry, but he also couldn't ignore his mother looming in the distance. She had to be blowing up his phone with calls and texts, but he didn't know because he still hadn't turned it on. She would take all of it out on him as soon as he returned, and that thought was enough to make him wonder if homelessness would be better.

Maybe he could stay in his tiger form and hang around the park he'd seen yesterday after Jordan and Farley had made him climb out of the trunk. He didn't want to assume that Farley and his parents would want him around all the time or that they would allow him to move in, but he dreaded going back.

The smell of food hit his nose, and his stomach grumbled. Farley heard it and grinned at him, and for the first time, Irwin allowed himself to do what felt natural and smiled back. It seemed to startle Farley, but his smile didn't vanish, so Irwin was sure he'd done the right thing.

"Good morning," he murmured as he walked into the kitchen.

"Irwin," Farley's mother said.

She came closer, and Irwin steeled himself for what was coming. He didn't expect the hug, but as soon as she wrapped her arms around him, he melted in the embrace.

He couldn't remember the last time anyone, let alone a mother, had hugged him. His mother certainly didn't, and even though he'd only met Farley's mom yesterday, she'd already managed to make him feel welcome and like he mattered to her.

"I'm glad you and Farley found each other," she said as she stepped back. "I won't say that I'm not worried about how young you both are, but I'm sure you'll work things out. The important thing is that you found each other, right?"

Irwin nodded, unable to make his mouth work. Farley's mother looked and sounded almost happy at the thought that Irwin was her son's mate. It didn't make sense in Irwin's mind, and he didn't know how to deal with it.

"We're headed out," Farley's father said. "Please finish cleaning the kitchen before you leave, and we'll talk more tonight, Farley."

Farley nodded. Irwin waited, unsure of how Farley's father had taken the news, but he just patted Irwin's back and winked at him. Then he left with his mate behind him.

"That means he likes you," Farley said.

"It does?"

Farley nodded and opened the oven. "My dad doesn't talk a lot, but there are ways to tell that he cares about you. Like this, for example. He left a plate for you in the oven so it would still be warm when you were ready to eat."

Irwin was overwhelmed. He pressed his lips together and told himself he wasn't going to cry, but he wasn't sure he could resist. He didn't think anyone had ever done anything for him as nice as what Farley's father had done this morning. He cared about Irwin, even though he barely knew him, while Irwin's mother couldn't care less. How was Irwin supposed to deal with that?

Farley gently touched Irwin's shoulder. "Why don't you sit down and eat? We can talk once you're feeling better."

Irwin nodded. He couldn't speak, so he might as well eat.

He flopped onto a chair and went to work. It was a normal breakfast, just bacon and eggs with toast, but it was delicious. Irwin's mother controlled what he ate with the excuse of not wanting him to get fat, and he couldn't remember the last time he'd had bacon or whole eggs. When she cooked for him, she only gave him the egg whites.

"So as I'm sure you've noticed, I still live with my parents," Farley explained. "I graduated from high school recently, and I've been trying to figure out what I want to do with the rest of my life since then. So far, I've come up empty, and I'm a bit worried, but my parents aren't. They told me I can continue living with them for as long as I want, but I need to contribute."

Irwin nodded. It made sense but also made him feel guilty because he wasn't doing anything to contribute to pride life. He spent most of his time in his room, and when he didn't, most people didn't want him around. They all wanted to forget he existed, including his mother.

"I'm trying to find a job," Farley continued. "There's not a lot in a town so small, but I'm sure I'll find something. Once I do, I can focus more on the future. I don't know if I want to go to college, but there's nothing that jumps out at me, so I guess I'll see. I plan to continue living with my parents for a while, anyway."

So they wouldn't be moving in together. Irwin wasn't surprised, but he was a bit disappointed. It wasn't fair to expect Farley to be his way out of the nightmare his life was, though. Irwin had never felt strong enough to stand up for himself, but maybe knowing what was waiting for him out here, knowing the future he and Farley could have, would give him the boost he needed. He was still terrified of his mother and wasn't sure he'd ever be able to stand up to her, but there were ways around that.

Irwin's mother wasn't the pride's alpha. She might control Irwin's life, but that was it. If he went straight to the alpha, she wouldn't be able to do anything to stop him.

Farley's phone vibrated on the table. Farley snatched it up, looked at the screen, and answered. "Hey, Simon," he said.

Simon was talking loudly enough that Irwin would have been able to hear him even if he hadn't been a shifter.

"Irwin's gone. No one knows where he is, and his mother is freaking out. I know the two of you aren't bonded, but do you think you could still use your bond to find him? Or maybe shimmer to him?"

"Calm down," Farley said.

"How can I calm down? A member of our pride has vanished. He's your mate, Farley. How can *you* be so calm?"

"He's sitting in front of me at my kitchen table."

There was a moment of silence, and Farley took the opportunity to put the phone on speaker and place it on the table.

"Really?" Simon asked.

Irwin wasn't sure he'd ever spoken to Simon, but it was time to start. "I'm sorry," he quickly said. "I should have told someone I was leaving the house yesterday. I didn't want to worry anyone but didn't realize I'd be gone so long." He hadn't planned at all when he'd left the house. He'd just wanted to get away.

Simon sighed. "It's fine. I can't say I blame you for needing space, but you should come home. Your mother is freaking out, and that's never a good thing. Gal knows that you're gone, too, and he's worried."

"I'll be there as soon as I can," Irwin promised.

His goal had never been to make people worry about him, not even his mother. He'd just wanted to be free for one day, and he had been. Now, it was time to go back.

He looked at Farley.

He might be going back, but that didn't mean he'd stay there.

CHAPTER FOUR

Farley could see the happiness draining from Irwin's expression. He'd been fine earlier, if a bit awkward, but now that he had to go home, all of it was gone. It was clear he wanted to stay, but he couldn't. Farley didn't think he'd say yes even if he offered.

But maybe Irwin didn't realize he didn't have to do this on his own. He'd never have to do any of this on his own again because he had Farley now.

As soon as they hung up with Simon, Irwin started cleaning up the kitchen. He was silent and focused on his task, and Farley watched him for a moment. He wanted to do so much for his mate, but he didn't know where to start beyond being by his side when he faced his mother. It wouldn't be pleasant, but he couldn't allow her to treat Irwin the way she had since Irwin was a child. It might not be Farley's place to say anything about it, but he felt it was because of who he was to Irwin.

The council laws were clear when it came to mates. Even if they weren't bonded, no one could interfere. That meant that if Irwin's mother tried keeping Irwin and Farley apart, Farley could go to the enforcers and have them step in. That was even without considering the abuse, and Farley had every intention of making sure that was over. He just wasn't sure how Irwin would react to his stepping in.

Farley didn't know if Irwin loved his mother, but he probably did. He'd stayed this entire time, allowing her to hurt him. Farley didn't know much about abuse and how people reacted to it, but it was clear this wouldn't be easy for Irwin. Farley didn't want to make things even harder on him, but he didn't know where to start helping him.

He was only nineteen and still lived with his parents. Even if he could ask Irwin to move in with them, he wasn't sure it was the right thing to do. He desperately wanted to shield Irwin from his mother and everything else that had been happening in the house, but part of him wondered if he should.

He would do it if no one else intervened, but there was someone whose job it was to keep people safe and who hadn't done anything yet. Simon had said the alpha was worried because Irwin wasn't home, but why was he worried now but hadn't been when Irwin's mother had been abusing him? Farley wasn't sure how to behave when it came to alphas and all that stuff, but he wouldn't hesitate to tell Gal what he thought of the way he'd ignored Irwin's pain if things came to that.

"I'm going to go upstairs to change. Can you call Simon back and ask him to pick me up?" Irwin asked quietly.

Farley blinked. He'd been so deep in his thoughts that he hadn't realized Irwin was done with the kitchen. He felt guilty because his father had asked him to clean up, but it was too late to do anything now.

He got up. "We're both going to change, and I'll shimmer you there."

Irwin's eyes widened. "You don't have to do that. My mother might see you if you take me back."

"That's kind of the point. I *want* her to see me. I don't know if you're ready to tell her we're mates, but I think it would be the best thing to do right now."

"She's going to be so angry if I tell her. I don't want her to yell at you."

Farley grinned. "I don't care if she yells at me. It's not going to keep me away from you. Nothing will."

Irwin stared at him as if he didn't quite believe what he

was saying—he probably didn't. He wasn't used to having people on his side who wanted him to succeed and be happy. The only person he'd ever had was his mother, and she wanted to keep him where he was so she could continue controlling him.

Not Farley. Farley wanted his mate to be happy, even if it meant that Irwin wasn't in his life. It would hurt, but as long as Irwin had what he wanted, Farley was ready to take a step back.

He moved in front of Irwin and touched his shoulder. "I can come back here right away if that's what you want, but I'd really like it if you allowed me to stay with you. I already know she's not going to be easy to deal with. I talked to her twice, and she yelled at me both times. I don't want you to go back alone."

"I appreciate what you're doing, but I don't need you to stick around. She won't hurt me."

Farley suspected that she would. He'd seen how she hadn't hesitated to slap Irwin the night of the party, and he didn't think it was the only time she'd done that. It wouldn't be the last if no one stopped her, and Irwin didn't seem to be capable of doing that. Farley didn't want to make things worse with his presence, but he wouldn't allow anyone to hurt his mate if he could stop them.

There was a fine line between allowing Irwin the freedom of saying yes or no to his presence and not wanting him to be hurt. Farley didn't know if he was walking that line the right way, and he didn't want to force Irwin into anything, but he needed him to understand.

He chose his words carefully. "I realize you probably don't want me to see how bad things are with your mother, and I won't be able to ignore it if I come with you this morning. I've already seen how things are, though. I saw it the night of the party, and I'm sorry if this is too much for you or if you think

I'm an asshole, but I won't let her hurt you again. I'm only a Nix, and I have no doubt that she's stronger than me, but it won't stop me from trying to protect you."

Irwin's eyes were wide as he looked up at Farley. "I don't want you to be hurt. I don't know what she'll do to you if you stand up to her. No one ever has."

Farley couldn't deny he was worried. Irwin and his mother were tiger shifters, and it would be easy for her to hurt him. He couldn't shift into anything to defend himself. His only defense was to shimmer away, but he wouldn't do so without Irwin.

He thought about what Jordan had suggested yesterday. It had felt like going behind Irwin's back then, but it wouldn't be a betrayal if he could convince Irwin to go along with it. "Jordan said yesterday that we should talk to your alpha, and after Simon mentioned him earlier, I think Jordan was right."

Irwin started shaking his head, but he quickly stopped and frowned. "You think he'll do something to my mother?"

"I know he's not like your old alpha, so he'll probably try to make her stop. I don't know what he can do or what he's willing to do. I've never had a pride, so I'm out of my depth."

Farley had never even had a real tribe. Both his parents had decided they wanted to be together and had left their tribes because their people hadn't been happy with that decision, which meant that Farley had grown up without a family other than his parents. He had friends like Miko, and Miko's parents had become a sort of family, but it wasn't the same as a tribe. Besides, a tribe wasn't like a pride, anyway. Farley had no idea what he was doing, but maybe he didn't have to.

"I heard Gal is a nice person," Irwin said.

"Both Jordan and Simon suggested that you should talk to him, and I trust them. They know him better than either of us, and if they say this is the right thing to do, I think it probably is. At the very least, Gal should know what your mother's been up to in his pride."

Irwin still appeared hesitant, but they didn't have a lot of time to think about it. They needed to go, and they needed to do so before Irwin's mother decided to do something stupid.

Hell, maybe they wouldn't have to tell Gal what had been happening. Maybe whatever was going on at the house right now would be enough for him to realize how bad a person Irwin's mother was. It was clear Irwin didn't want to admit to his alpha what had been happening, and Farley didn't want him to have to do anything he wasn't comfortable with.

But he couldn't shield Irwin from this, no matter how much he wanted to. Life was uncomfortable sometimes, and they'd both have to deal with it the best they could.

Irwin didn't want to talk to the alpha. He didn't want to admit what he'd been going through and how he'd allowed his mother to hurt him. He didn't want to appear weak.

Even though he was.

He truly didn't understand why fate had thought it was a good idea to choose him as a mate for Farley. Farley deserved someone stronger, but unfortunately, there was no way for them to change any of this. They were mates, and that was that.

Thankfully, Farley didn't seem to hate the idea of them being together. Irwin certainly didn't, even though he knew he came with a lot of problems. If he wanted to be with Farley and deserve him, he needed to make changes, and the first of those was to deal with his mother. Once she couldn't hurt him anymore and her control over him was gone, he could change his life and make him worth it to his mate.

He and Farley went upstairs to change. The only clothes Irwin had belonged to Jordan, but when he reached for them, Farley shook his head and grabbed more of his clothes to give him. He was taller than Irwin, but thankfully, not by much. His jeans were too long but didn't fall off Irwin's body, and he felt good wearing them. He wasn't sure Farley realized how much stronger Irwin felt just from wearing one of his sweaters and jeans. They carried his mate's scent, and being able to smell Farley made Irwin feel stronger and safer.

Just what he needed to face his mother.

Irwin could have talked to Gal a long time ago. After the alpha had taken over the pride and settled in, it would have been fairly easy to sneak up to the roof and around the house to his office. Irwin hadn't done it because he'd been afraid of his mother's reaction, but also because he knew there was a chance she'd be kicked out of the pride. She and Kevin had been lucky they'd been allowed to stay after what had happened with Simon, but this would probably mean she'd be kicked out, and Irwin didn't know how to feel about that.

She was his mother, and he didn't want her to be without a home and a pride, but he realized that she didn't deserve to be a pride member. She wasn't a bully just to him. Things had improved after Gal took over, but before, she'd bullied anyone who wasn't in her small group of friends. She was more cautious now, and she'd turned more of her attention to Irwin, but she was still the same person she'd been then, and Irwin didn't think she would ever change.

But she was still his mother, and doing this was hard for him. It was a choice he needed to make, though. Be honest and talk to Gal, tell him what his mother had been doing, or lose Farley.

That was one thing he wasn't ready to do. He didn't know what things would be like between them, but he wanted to find out. He wanted to give their bond a chance.

And that wouldn't be possible with his mother in the picture.

"Ready?" Farley asked once they were both dressed.

Catherine Lievens

Irwin wasn't, and he didn't think he ever would be, but he nodded anyway. He had a choice between his mother and his future, and he didn't have to think about which way to go. It was as easy as that. Farley was his future and the only thing that was right in his world.

He wasn't giving it up.

Farley took Irwin's hand and pulled him toward the stairs. Irwin marveled at the easy touch and wondered if Farley knew he'd done it. Maybe to him, it was normal to touch other people, but it had been a long time since Irwin had had anyone touch him the way Farley and his family had. Farley's mother had hugged Irwin so easily this morning. Irwin wanted more of that. He wanted a family and people he could be himself with. He wanted friends who would hug him. He wanted Farley to hold his hand every day.

To have those things, he needed to be brave. He needed the truth to come out and to admit that he'd been a victim.

He straightened his back. If it had been anyone else in his place, he wouldn't have viewed them as a victim. If anyone else had been standing up to his mother and telling the alpha how much she hurt them, Irwin would have been in awe of how brave they were. Why couldn't he feel that way about himself? After so many years, he was finally strong enough to stand up to his mother. Surely, that was something to be proud of.

They stepped out on the porch, and Irwin shivered. He found himself leaning closer to Farley without meaning to, but Farley didn't seem to have a problem with it. He smiled at him and wrapped an arm around his shoulders, and for a moment, Irwin allowed himself to believe that they were going on a date rather than to talk to his mother.

"It's going to be fine," Farley promised.

Irwin was about to tell him he wasn't sure about that, but Farley interrupted him in the best way possible. Irwin hadn't expected it, and when Farley's lips landed on his, he was shocked speechless.

He'd been dreaming of this moment his entire life. He'd come close to having his first kiss once, but his mother had walked in just before it happened. He'd never been kissed before today, and now that he had a taste of Farley, he knew there was no way he could give him up.

The kiss wasn't deep. It was just a press of their lips, but it gave Irwin a taste of Farley. At that moment, he was surrounded by his mate, and he could imagine the rest of his life being like this. He desperately wanted it.

He wanted to be able to kiss Farley whenever he wanted and to do other things with him. He wanted to explore life and the world in a way he'd never been allowed to, and he couldn't imagine himself doing it without his mate.

He didn't know if he could have been brave enough to stand up to his mother before, but he was now because not doing so meant losing his mate, and that wasn't something he could allow.

Farley leaned back. He was smiling slightly, and Irwin couldn't stop staring at him.

"Did I distract you?" Farley asked.

Irwin frowned. "Is that why you did it?"

"And because I wanted to. Was it okay?"

"Yes. You can distract me whenever you want."

Farley laughed. "I might have to find another way, because I doubt people will want to watch me kiss you all day. How about you hold my hand instead? It might not distract you, but it'll be enough for you to know I'm standing beside you and not going anywhere."

Farley stepped away from Irwin, and Irwin realized that he'd shimmered them in front of the pride house. He held out a hand, and Irwin didn't hesitate to take it. His skin crawled as he thought of the possibility that his mother was watching them through a window, but he ignored it, even though it wasn't easy. This was his life now, and his mother could either stop controlling him or vanish from his life.

She might not have a choice after he talked to Gal.

Irwin felt stronger with Farley by his side. He led the way inside the house, hoping they'd be able to reach Gal's office before anyone noticed them. He didn't know what kind of mess his mother had started when she'd realized he was gone yesterday, but he wasn't looking forward to finding out. Nothing was ever easy or nice when it came to her.

"What the hell do you think you're doing?" a woman's voice asked as soon as Irwin and Farley stepped into the house.

Irwin's back went ramrod straight, and he almost groaned. He'd hoped they could reach Gal's office, but apparently, his mother had been waiting for him in the entrance, probably looking out the window to see when he arrived like he'd been afraid of.

And she didn't sound happy.

Farley didn't have to look to know who the woman screeching at them was. Even if he'd never met her before, he would have known it was Irwin's mother from her voice.

Irwin had cringed a bit when she appeared from the corner of the room by the window. Had she been spying on them? Had she seen Farley kiss Irwin?

Farley stood up straighter. He didn't care if she had. He wasn't ashamed of his mate or of wanting him. They were both adults, and Irwin's mother had nothing to say about their relationship that Farley would care about.

He was worried about her words but even more about what she was about to do. Every movement she made told Farley she was beyond angry, and he'd already seen her like this once before on the night of the party. She'd hit Irwin then, but he'd been alone, and Farley had arrived too late to help him. That wouldn't be so today. If Irwin's mother thought she would hit him, she'd get a nasty surprise when she realized that Farley wasn't going anywhere. He didn't care how much she screamed. He wasn't afraid of her.

Not much, anyway.

She stopped in front of them and raised her hand.

Farley moved quickly, placing himself in front of Irwin. He wasn't surprised when she dropped her hand without hitting him. She was used to Irwin taking whatever she handed out without saying a word, but Farley wasn't going to do that. If she as much as touched him, he wouldn't hesitate to go to her alpha.

"You," she said, the word full of loathing and disgust.

Farley grinned at her. "Yep, it's me again. I see you haven't become any nicer."

"I told you to stay away from my son. What are you doing to him?"

Irwin was still silent. Farley had hoped he would stand up to his mother, but he understood why it was hard for him. After so many years of being controlled by her, it was normal for him to retreat into his mind and allow her to say and do whatever she wanted. Farley didn't need Irwin to protect him, anyway. He could do that himself and had every intention of doing so.

"I'm not doing anything to your son that he isn't okay with."

She turned incredibly red. "My son would never allow you to touch him in any way."

Her tone said that she'd seen Farley kiss Irwin earlier. It was a small miracle that she hadn't charged outside and interrupted them. Maybe she hadn't had time to do so, or maybe she'd expected Irwin to come into the house alone. She would probably have hurt him if he had, but now she couldn't. She'd have to take out her anger on someone else, and Farley wondered if that someone else would be him. He didn't care if she attempted to slap him as long as she didn't shift. He just didn't want to become tiger chow.

"Your son allowed me to kiss him, and I'm pretty sure he wants me to do it again. You don't have a say in our relationship."

Farley wondered if her head might be about to explode. Her color turned from a deep red to an almost purple, as if she was having trouble breathing. Maybe this was how Farley would solve the problem for his mate. Maybe he'd kill his mother with his words.

He didn't want Irwin to lose her, but he doubted she'd still be in Irwin's life by the end of it. As far as Farley was concerned, that would be good riddance, but he understood that Irwin might not feel that way.

"What have you done to my son? You've taken advantage of him and how vulnerable and young he is. I'm going to report you. I'm sure the enforcers will want to know what you've been up to."

Farley wasn't sure how to deal with Irwin's mother. His own mother was nice and loving, and she would never have even thought about hitting him. Irwin's mother didn't seem to be going that way for now, maybe because she thought her threats would be enough to make him run.

Instead, he laughed. "You can call the enforcers. I'm sure they'd like to know how you've been treating your son all these years. And just so you know, Irwin might be young, but I'm seven years younger than him, so that excuse won't work. I haven't taken advantage of him. That was you, lady."

Farley was getting angry. He didn't like feeling that way, but it was on Irwin's behalf, so he could deal with it.

She spluttered, and for a moment, Farley thought she was

about to hit him. He should have known better. Her target had always been her son, and this time wasn't any different.

She darted around Farley, pushing him aside. He hadn't expected it, so he stumbled and had to let go of Irwin. That was enough for her to reach him, and she raised her hand high, slapping him on the cheek. Farley cried out, but Irwin barely reacted. He stumbled back a step, then just stood there, staring at her as she raised her arm again.

Irwin's gaze was vacant as if he'd retreated into his mind. He'd also looked like this the night of the birthday party, and Farley suspected it was how he dealt with his mother's violence. It was easier for him when he wasn't entirely there.

Farley didn't blame him, but he wouldn't allow him to be hurt. He didn't care if Irwin's mother turned her anger toward him. He could take it.

He grabbed her wrist and pulled her backward. She screamed as if he was killing her, and he quickly let go of her. He realized it had been the wrong thing to do when she turned to him, ready to slap him instead of her son. He grabbed her wrist, but she was already raising her other hand, and she wouldn't miss him.

The slap never came because Irwin grabbed her. She was stuck with Farley holding one of her hands and Irwin holding the other. She screamed again, and Farley let go. Irwin did the same, and Farley grabbed him and dragged him into his arms, tucking him against his side to protect him.

He hadn't expected Irwin to react to what was happening. He'd done nothing when his mother had hurt him, but as soon as she'd turned her anger toward Farley, he'd stepped in. He wouldn't stand up for himself, but he would do so for Farley, and Farley was touched. It was clear he mattered to Irwin, and while they still had to work out many things, Farley was convinced they'd make it.

They had to. They were mates for a reason.

"How dare you touch me?" Irwin's mother asked, circling around them as if she was trying to get to Irwin again.

She probably was. She might be a stubborn asshole, but Farley would out-stubborn her. When it came to protecting Irwin, he was ready to do pretty much anything.

She took another step forward. "He's mine, and I won't allow you to take him away," she said, a terrifying expression twisting her face. "You haven't seen anything, but Irwin knows. He knows what I'll do because of this. You should turn and run while you're still in time, boy. If you don't want me to destroy you, you'll walk out the door right now and never come back."

Okay, maybe Farley *could* understand why Irwin hadn't stood up to her before. She was terrifying. He was pretty sure he'd seen her eyes shift to her tiger's eyes for a second, and while she seemed to have herself under control, Farley couldn't tell if it would last. The thought of what she could do to him made him want to turn and run, but he wasn't leaving Irwin on his own.

"I'm not going anywhere. I won't allow you to hurt Irwin ever again, and I don't care that you're his mother. What you've been doing to him isn't right, and someone has to stop you."

She laughed. "And you think you're going to be the one to do that? You're nothing more than a child. There's nothing you can do to me."

"There might be nothing *he* can do, but the same doesn't go for me," a strong male voice boomed behind her.

Irwin almost laughed at the way his mother paled when she heard Gal's voice. Her color vanished so quickly that he wondered if she was about to faint, especially when she stumbled as she turned around to face the alpha.

Gal stood at the bottom of the stairs, staring her down. He barely looked at Farley and Irwin, and Irwin was grateful for that. His legs were shaking, and his knees felt like they might not continue keeping him upright for long.

As soon as he'd realized his mother was there, he'd started to shut down. He was so used to reacting like that he couldn't stop it. For years, it had been the only way for him to withstand his mother's abuse, and his body and mind went there automatically as soon as his mother started screaming.

He'd heard what Farley said and felt the slap his mother had landed on his cheek. It had stung, but he was used to the feeling.

It was when his mother had tried hitting Farley that Irwin had finally snapped out of it. It was one thing for her to hurt him, but he would never let her or anyone else raise a hand to Farley. Farley was precious, and no one was allowed to hurt him.

Irwin had seen the shock in his mother's gaze when he'd stepped in, but it hadn't been enough to stop her. She always got what she wanted, or at least she had before. It was clear things were changing. Irwin had stood up to her, and Gal had caught her red-handed. There was no way for any of them to know how long he'd been standing there, but if Irwin had to guess, he'd say that Gal had heard most of what his mother had said.

And he was pissed.

His expression was serious, but Irwin could see the anger in his gaze. He looked like he wanted to grab Irwin's mother and drag her out of the house, but he wouldn't. From everything Irwin had heard, Gal was a good person and a good alpha, which meant he'd do this the right way.

Irwin swallowed and pressed closer to Farley. Farley didn't step away, thankfully. He tightened his arm around Irwin's shoulders and held him close as they watched Gal move toward Irwin's mother.

She lightly bowed her head and kept her gaze down. She might be a tiger shifter, but both she and her tiger knew that Gal was their alpha. They needed to obey his orders and respect him, which was why she wasn't screaming at him or turning around to leave.

Gal turned his attention to Irwin. Irwin almost whimpered, terrified of what the alpha had to say. They stared at each other for a moment, and Irwin couldn't look away. He didn't know what Gal saw in him and wasn't sure he wanted to find out.

"Are you all right?" Gal eventually asked.

Irwin nodded. "I'm fine. I'm sorry I didn't tell anyone that I was leaving yesterday. I should have called."

"You should have, but I've been clued in about many things I hadn't noticed before, and I can understand why you left. Just don't do it again, all right? If you need to go, at least tell Simon." His focus turned to Farley, then back to Irwin. "I suspect that we'll know where to find you next time. Why don't the two of you go to my office? I'll talk to your mother for a moment, then join you."

"Alpha—" Irwin's mother began, but one look from Gal made her snap her mouth shut.

She had always ranted against Gal and the kind of alpha he was, hating him because he wasn't a tiger and hadn't been part of their pride before becoming alpha, but when she was confronted by him, she couldn't say anything. He *was* her alpha. She didn't respect him, but that didn't change the power he had over her.

Gal turned his attention back to Irwin. "Please go. I'll be right there."

Irwin felt rooted in place, but thankfully, Farley was there. He gently pushed him forward, even though he had no idea where he was going.

The movement was enough to get Irwin to react. He took Farley's hand and dragged him forward, stepping into the hallway by the stairs. Both of them were silent. Irwin could hear Gal talking to his mother behind them and the sound of other people in the house, but none of that mattered.

Farley had stood up for him, and more importantly, *he* had stood up for Farley. He'd been ready to defend him in any way he had to, something he'd never been able to do for himself. He didn't know what he was ready for when it came to their relationship, but he wanted Farley in his life, and there wasn't a day he'd regret taking a chance on him.

Irwin wasn't surprised to find Simon at his desk when they reached the front office. He looked up with a frown, but it quickly vanished when he saw Irwin. He stood up and rushed around the desk, and Irwin was stunned when Simon wrapped him in his arms.

They'd never really talked before, and Irwin didn't understand why Simon seemed to care so much about him and his well-being. Was it because he'd seen Irwin's mother abuse him the night of the party? Whatever the reason, Irwin found he didn't care. He wanted friends. He wanted a family, a happy life with his mate, and everything else he'd never thought he could have.

He gently hugged Simon back, then stepped away.

"Sorry about that," Simon said. "I was really worried about you."

"You knew I was with Farley."

"I found out when he told me this morning, but I was still worried. I guess I didn't really believe you were all right until I saw you just now." He hesitated. "I and a few others wondered if your mother had done something to you, even though she was behaving like she was freaking out about your disappearance."

"She really was freaking out. She didn't know where I

was."

Simon nodded. "Good. She doesn't deserve to know where you are."

"I have to say I agree with that," Gal said as he strode into the front office. "She won't bother you for the rest of the day, but I can't make any promises for the future until you talk to me. Are you ready to do so, Irwin?"

Irwin wasn't. He wanted to drag Farley to his bedroom, lock the door, and hide from the rest of the world. He wouldn't be hiding alone anymore. He'd be hiding with his mate, and there was nothing better he could think of.

But Farley had friends and a family, and he didn't deserve to have to leave them all behind for Irwin. Irwin didn't want him to. He wanted to become part of Farley's life, not the other way around. He didn't have a life for Farley to become part of, but he could change that, and he would.

"I think it's time," he agreed.

Gal nodded. "Good. Step into my office. Simon, can you bring us something to drink? Have the two of you eaten this morning?"

"We had breakfast at my place," Farley said, stepping forward. "I'm Farley."

"One of Jordan's friends, right?"

It was obvious that Gal wanted to ask if Farley was anything more than that—he and Irwin were holding hands. The alpha didn't, though. It made Irwin respect him a little bit more. He wasn't pushing for answers but rather giving everyone time and space to tell him whatever they needed to say.

"He's Jordan's friend, but he's also my mate," Irwin murmured.

Gal didn't seem surprised. "Congratulations to both of you."

Irwin felt like he was in an alternate reality. Everyone was so nice to him, and Gal had stopped his mother from hurting him. Those things had never happened before, and Irwin wasn't sure how to deal with them.

He didn't have to until he was sitting in Gal's office with Gal sitting on the edge of his desk.

"You should have come to me sooner," Gal said gently. "When I took over the pride, I knew it would be complicated, but I didn't realize just how many problems I'd have to deal with. If I'd known your mother was abusive, I would have intervened much sooner."

"I think I didn't realize just how abusive she was until recently. It was so normal for me that I didn't think there was anything I could do to change it." Irwin hated that, but it was over, and now, he could focus on his future.

"I'm angry at myself for not seeing it sooner and because no one here helped you. But that's over now. Please, if you have any problems, come to me or Simon. You can even talk to Forest. I understand you might not be comfortable with either of us, but I don't want you to keep secrets like this anymore."

Farley was still holding Irwin's hand, and Irwin squeezed it, needing the anchor. "My life has changed a lot over the past few days. I promise to come to you if I have any problem, though. I trust you."

Irwin really did. He hadn't known what to think of the alpha before, but Gal had stepped in right away when Irwin had needed him. It made sense that Irwin's mother didn't like him. Now that he knew of this mess, he would fix it, and it wouldn't go well for her.

Irwin didn't care anymore. The only person he cared about was Farley, and he was safe.

CHAPTER FIVE

"What do you think of this one?" Farley asked as he looked around the empty living room.

Irwin stood next to him, doing the same. Farley didn't know how to read his expression, but he felt he should try, because he wasn't sure Irwin would tell him the truth. Did he really like the apartment, or was he saying he did because he thought Farley was annoyed at having to look for a place for him to live? Farley suspected the latter.

So far, Irwin had liked every apartment they'd visited, even when there had been something glaringly wrong with it, like the one where it had sounded like a family of elephants lived next door. Farley had never heard anyone make that much noise. The realtor had assured them the couple only had two children, but Farley wasn't sure he could believe that. There was no way two kids made that much noise. Right?

"I like it," Irwin said.

Farley narrowed his eyes at him. "Do you really like it, or are you just saying that because you think it's what I want to hear? Because I don't mind shimmering you around town to look at more apartments." Even though this was the fifth today, Farley desperately wanted to move on to something else.

Irwin looked away, but that didn't mean he was lying. He usually avoided looking Farley in the eyes, something Farley suspected he'd learned to deal with his mother. If he didn't look at her, he might be able to keep her calm.

Farley wasn't like her. He wanted Irwin to look at him, but he also knew that pushing him wouldn't help. He was still finding his way in the world without his mother, and it wasn't easy.

She still lived with the pride. From what Farley had been told, she'd been forbidden from talking to Irwin, and so far, she'd obeyed that order. Farley had heard from Simon that she was loudly unhappy about that, but Irwin hadn't spent much time at the house, anyway. He spent more time with Farley than in the bedroom that had been his only home for his entire life.

Farley liked being Irwin's anchor, the one place where he could go when his life was a mess, but he wanted to do well by him. It wasn't healthy for Irwin to hide from his past and his mother. When Gal had suggested Irwin find an apartment outside the pride house, Farley jumped on the opportunity to go with him.

He leaned his shoulder against the wall and watched his mate. "You know that if you don't want to move out, Gal isn't going to force you to, right?"

"I don't want to continue living at the house," Irwin said quickly, as if he was afraid Farley would take away the opportunity to find him an apartment.

Farley would never do that. Besides, this apartment didn't hinge on him. Gal had clearly noticed that Irwin was uncomfortable at the house, and when he'd told him to find an apartment, he'd said that the pride would buy and furnish it. Irwin was a pride member, and the pride was responsible for his well-being. That hadn't worked well for the first twenty-six years, but hopefully, it was over now. Gal was doing what he could to make Irwin more comfortable, but it was obvious that would never happen as long as he stayed at the house.

There were too many bad memories there, and not only of Irwin's mother. The rest of the pride had never treated Irwin well, and the thought of it made Farley angry. Sometimes, he had to resist the urge to snap at Nestor and Simon, even though they'd both apologized to Irwin. What had happened to Irwin wasn't their fault, and it wasn't fair to hold any of it against them, especially considering how young Jordan was. He was just one year older than Farley, and at twenty, it wasn't a surprise that he hadn't noticed that someone he wasn't friends with was being abused. Simon was older, but from what Farley knew, he'd done his best to stay away from Irwin's mother and her friends, and he'd been right, considering what Kevin had done to him.

"And I do like this apartment," Irwin continued.

"That's good. What do you like about it?"

It was always hard for Irwin to assert himself, and Farley wasn't quite sure how to help him. He'd found that asking Irwin his opinion made it easier for him to speak up, even though he often looked almost ashamed to tell Farley how he felt and why he felt that way.

But not today. Today, he stepped closer to the window and smiled. "I can see the park from here."

He could. For some reason, he was fascinated by the park. It probably had to do with the fact that his mother had kept him locked up in the house for so long. He needed freedom, yet at the same time, he was afraid of it. The park would be a good compromise, and if he wanted to live across the street from it, then Farley didn't have a problem with it.

Farley moved closer and pressed a hand to the small of Irwin's back. Irwin shivered like he always did when Farley touched him. He wasn't used to this, either. He'd never had casual touches, and Farley wanted to give him more of those. He wanted to give his mate more of everything he'd missed out on.

"I do like the view," he said.

Irwin tilted his head back slightly and smiled at him. "Do you think Gal would be okay with this one?"

"The two of you are adorable," the realtor said from the

corner of the room.

Farley had almost forgotten she was there. He gave her a tight smile, then turned his attention back to Irwin. "He said you could choose whatever apartment you want, and he was serious. If this is the one, then it's the one."

"It's not the most expensive one, right?" Irwin asked, looking worried.

Considering how guilty Gal felt that he hadn't noticed what Irwin was going through, Farley was pretty sure the alpha would offer to buy him a mansion if that was what Irwin asked for. It wasn't. Even though they'd looked at other bigger and more luxurious apartments, Irwin wanted this one. Farley could see it in the way he behaved.

"It's not the most expensive one," the realtor confirmed, looking in her notebook.

She was a nice woman who'd been doing her best to give Irwin what he was looking for even though he didn't dare ask for it. So far, she'd been professional, but Farley had seen she had a soft spot for Irwin, so he wasn't surprised that she found him adorable. Farley couldn't deny Irwin was. He wanted to wrap his mate in a blanket and carry him home to his bedroom.

He wasn't the only one who wanted to protect Irwin. Irwin seemed to create that feeling in many people, and the realtor had taken a shine to him as soon as she'd met them.

"If this is the place you want, then Gal is going to buy it for you," Farley assured Irwin. "And once you're ready to move on, it will still belong to the pride, so you don't have to worry about that. He told you to choose whatever place you felt more comfortable in. If this is this place, you just have to say it."

Irwin was hesitant, but he nodded. "I *really* like it."

"It will be perfect for the two of you. There's no one I like finding homes for more than young couples," the realtor said.

"Oh, we're not moving in together," Farley told her. "This apartment is for Irwin."

The realtor frowned, then nodded. "I apologize. If you like this one, I'm going to put everything together and send an email to your alpha."

Gal had been the one who'd contacted her, and even though Irwin was choosing the apartment, he was in charge of everything else. He just needed to know what Irwin liked, and Farley was pretty sure that Irwin would be allowed to move in soon. Gal would make sure of it.

He looked around again. He liked the place, even though it was small. Irwin didn't need anything more. The one-bedroom apartment was perfect for him.

Especially with that view.

The realtor stepped away, leaving Farley and Irwin alone. Farley started to move away from his mate so he could poke his nose around a little longer, but Irwin grabbed his hand. He sucked in a breath, and Farley waited to see what his mate wanted.

"We could, you know," Irwin squeaked.

"We could what?"

Irwin turned to look at Farley. "Move in together. We could both move into this apartment."

Irwin knew that suggesting they move in together had been a bad idea right after the words left his mouth. Farley had been clear that they needed space and time to discover who they were and what they wanted in life. He'd been pushing Irwin to take more steps in that direction than Irwin ever had, and Irwin had hoped it would be enough. Farley cared about him, but it was obvious from his expression that his answer would be no.

Irwin quickly stepped back. "I'm sorry. I know I shouldn't

have suggested that and that it's too much, especially with the situation with my mother."

Because who would want to be stuck with that? Farley had been nothing but nice, but it had to grate on his nerves to have to deal with Irwin's mother. Thankfully, she'd been staying away since Gal had talked to her, but Irwin didn't fool himself that it would last forever. Eventually, Gal's focus would slip, and she'd take the opportunity to barge her way back into Irwin's life.

That was why Irwin was so eager to move out. As long as he lived under the same roof as her, he wouldn't actually be free. With this apartment, he'd have a chance at building a real life, and that was all he wanted.

That, and his mate.

He'd thought that he and Farley could do this together, but it was too soon. Irwin was a hot mess and didn't want to spill his problems into Farley's life. He shouldn't have offered for them to move in together, and he hoped Farley would behave as if he hadn't heard him.

He didn't. Of course he didn't.

"I don't think that's a good idea," Farley said gently. "You need to find out who you are as a person, and I don't believe you can do that if I'm here. You should have your own space and do whatever you want with it. You should be able to live without having to worry about anyone else, including me."

Irwin understood what he was saying and even knew why Farley was saying it. Farley was afraid that Irwin would become too dependent on him. He might not be wrong, but Irwin still wasn't sure why they couldn't move in together. Farley would eventually find a job and be out there doing his own thing, and surely Irwin would do the same. It wasn't like they'd spend every moment of every day together, even if they shared the apartment.

Even though Irwin partially understood Farley's decision,

this was another rejection in a long line of rejections. Irwin was used to them. He'd thought that maybe it was finally over, but he'd been wrong. He should have known better.

He should have known better about many things.

He needed out of the house, not only because his mother still lived there but also because of the way the other pride members treated him. He'd hoped things would get better with them once his mother was forced to step back, but it hadn't happened.

He'd managed to keep his secret for a long time, and not everyone believed that his mother had been abusing him. Some pride members thought that he was playing Gal, which was ridiculous because Gal wouldn't allow anyone to play him. Not everyone could see that, and some people thought Irwin was doing all this because he wanted an apartment and wanted the alpha to take care of him. They weren't entirely wrong. Irwin did want Gal to take care of him because he felt he deserved it. No one had ever helped him before, and he'd lived through hell for too long. Because no one had inter-vened, he'd never learned how to stand up on his own two feet. Maybe it was selfish of him to want help, but he didn't care if it was.

Irwin wasn't sure if he disliked those people the most or if that award went to the people who watched him with pity. He was sure that some of them had known his mother was abusing him, yet they'd never stepped in to help him. Now that it had come out, they wanted to talk and tell him how sorry they were.

Irwin didn't believe them.

They were trying to make themselves look like they were better than they actually were, and he didn't like that. He'd forgiven a handful of people, including Simon and Nestor, but that was where it ended. He couldn't forgive the others, especially the people who'd been adults and had known what was happening. They could have stopped all of it after Gal had become the alpha, but instead, they'd chosen to continue ignoring Irwin's pain. It was one more reason Irwin wanted out of the house, and he was glad he'd found a place to call home.

Even though it would be without Farley.

"I'm sorry," he whispered. "I shouldn't have suggested it. You already said you didn't want us to move in together. Forget it, all right?"

Irwin stepped away from Farley, but Farley stopped him. Irwin wanted to scream at him to let him go so he could lick his wound in peace, but Farley wouldn't. He always made sure Irwin understood what he was saying and how he felt. It was something Irwin usually liked because it meant he didn't have to guess, but right now, he wanted to be left alone for a few moments. He felt like he was about to start crying and didn't want to do that in front of his mate.

"You have nothing to be sorry about," Farley said. "It's normal that you don't want to live on your own. You never have because you've been with the pride your entire life. You probably don't know how to function without a bunch of people around you, but that's why it's important for you to do this."

"Because I need to find out who I am without my mother and everyone else," Irwin muttered.

Farley shuffled. "I'm repeating myself, aren't I?"

"A little bit."

Irwin knew this wasn't a rejection, but it felt like one, and he didn't like the way he wanted to curl up on himself and retreat into his mind. Farley wasn't hurting him. He was doing what he thought was best for Irwin and was probably right.

Irwin was seven years older than Farley. At twenty-six, he should have his life in order, or at the very least, he should have an idea of the direction in which he wanted it to go. Instead, he didn't know where to start. He had to learn everything about living on his own and so much more. He'd have to find a job, learn to pay taxes, cook, and so much more, and the thought was enough to make him want to scream in terror. How was he supposed to do this on his own? How was he supposed to become a productive adult when he'd been forbidden from being one his entire life?

"You're not going to be alone, even if you're the only one living here," Farley promised. "Besides, it's not forever. Eventually, we're going to move in together."

The thought made Irwin smile and lessened the burn of rejection. "Then maybe we should find something bigger."

Farley shook his head. "This is perfect. We won't need much space even when I move in with you. There are only two of us at the moment."

Irwin liked that Farley implied that wouldn't be so forever. They were both young, and considering the mess Irwin's life was, it was way too soon to think about bonding and children, but it was something they would talk about eventually.

Before, Irwin had decided not to have children because he hadn't wanted to bring even more people to his mother's abuse, but that was in the past. He could do whatever he wanted.

He just needed to find out what that was. That was going to be the hard part, especially because Irwin would have to do it on his own.

Dammit. Would it really be that bad to have Farley live with him? Irwin truly didn't understand why it was impossible. He could find out what he wanted from life and find a job, even with Farley living with him.

"I just don't see why we have to wait," he whined.

He doubted that anything Farley could say would change his mind about that. Waiting for them to move in together was a stupid idea.

Farley could see Irwin didn't understand. He didn't know how to explain things to him better, but he needed to try. He didn't want Irwin to feel like this was a rejection because it wasn't.

Farley wanted his mate. He wanted a life with him.

But to do that, they both needed to find a path they wanted to follow, and they wouldn't be able to do that if they focused on each other. They had to ditch their crutches to be independent, and that wouldn't work if they moved in together.

"We can't rely on each other too much," he explained. "Which is what we'll do if we move in together. Gal has already promised to pay your utilities and everything else you might need for as long as you need it, and I'm afraid I'd be relying on that, too. I can't afford that. We both need to decide what we want to do in life and find a job instead of allowing people to support us."

Farley felt the urgency, especially now that he had Irwin. He wanted to take care of his mate, but he couldn't do it if he continued living with his parents without doing anything. He was glad they'd given him time to think about his future, but unfortunately, it hadn't helped. He still didn't know what he wanted.

But he knew what he needed.

A job. Something where he could earn money to take care of Irwin, even though Irwin would soon be able to take care of himself. He could start putting money away for when they would move in together. That was as far as Farley allowed himself to think, but there were decades waiting for them, and they needed to set the foundation of them the right way. It had to be solid and right.

"I don't feel that it's a bad thing," Irwin argued. "We

already know we both need to find a job. Having someone who pays for what I need isn't going to change that. I'm not going to let Gal support me for the rest of my life. I know people think I'm weird and unable to take care of myself, but that's not true."

Farley was surprised at the strength in Irwin's voice. He liked it, just like he liked the fact that Irwin was asserting himself. He truly believed they should move in together, and it was tempting to say yes, but Farley needed to think this through.

"It's not only about you. I need to find my path in life, and I feel that living with you will distract me too much. I want to focus on you and our bond, and that's how things should be, but before we can focus on each other, we need to focus on ourselves. We need to start our life together on the best foot, and you have to experience being independent after spending so much time under your mother's thumb. She's never allowed you to do anything, but now, the world is yours. I don't want to keep you back."

"You wouldn't."

Irwin sounded grumbly, almost like a pouting child. This was a new side of him, too, and it was too adorable for words.

Farley pulled Irwin into his arms. "I promise this doesn't mean we won't see each other. I'll probably spend as much time with you as you spend time with me right now."

"Then wouldn't it be better to move in together?"

Farley laughed. It seemed that his Irwin was stubborn when he really wanted something. "How about we talk about it in a couple months? That way, you'll have time to settle into this apartment and your new life, but it won't be long. We'll celebrate Christmas and New Year's Eve and then talk about moving in together."

It was November, so it really wouldn't be long. Farley wasn't sure this was a good idea, but it felt right, especially when it made Irwin smile the way he was smiling up at him now.

"I'm just scared that you'll realize how messy my life is and that you'll decide it's too much for you," Irwin confessed.

It made sense. Irwin had been hurt by the one person who should have loved and cherished him and more importantly, protected him. The most important person in his life had hurt him for years in a way Irwin would never be able to forget. It was the only kind of relationship he knew. The entire time, he'd worked hard to keep his mother happy, and now, he was trying to do the same with Farley. He felt that if Farley wasn't happy, he'd leave him.

Farley needed him to understand that wasn't so.

"Our relationship won't be easy," he said. "We'll fight, and sometimes, we'll yell at each other. We'll make each other unhappy and angry."

"That sounds bad," Irwin said. His eyes were wide.

"It is, but it doesn't mean our relationship won't work. Even people who love each other fight and yell. Just know that I'll never hurt you, even if I'm angry. I realize that you probably can't trust that promise because your mother should never have hurt you, yet she did, but I'll do everything I can to show you I'm not lying. I never want you to be afraid of me or to be afraid of losing me. Unless you kill someone or something like that, I'm not going anywhere. You're my future. We're just taking a little time to start it, all right?"

Irwin was still pouty, but he nodded, and Farley was pretty sure he could see in his expression that he finally believed him.

He hadn't been lying when he'd said this wouldn't be easy. Irwin's past and the way he'd been hurt would complicate things, but Farley had faith in them. He knew they could do this, and they'd come out of this mess stronger than ever.

Together.

Now that Irwin had finally agreed with him, Farley looked around again. "So this is your new place?"

"Yeah." Irwin looked out the window at the trees. "As long as you like it, too. If you're eventually going to move in with me, I want you to feel at home here."

"I already do, because it's where you are."

Irwin's cheeks flushed, but he looked pleased. Farley wanted to see this kind of smile on his face more often, and he promised himself he'd do what he had to in order to make that happen.

His only goal in life couldn't be to make Irwin happy, but he felt like that might be so anyway. They were mates, which meant they'd make each other happy, be there for each other, and live life and its problems as a unit. In the end, that was all that mattered.

He leaned down to kiss Irwin. He was always careful because they hadn't talked about kissing and sex yet, and it was something else to add to their list of things to do. Thankfully, they had many years to discuss all of it.

Irwin was always okay with kissing. He'd even started initiating it, which had delighted Farley. Right now, though, Farley wanted to be the one to do this for Irwin. He needed Irwin to know that they'd always have each other whatever happened. Their bond would be stronger than any other relationship they'd have, as it should be.

When their lips met, Irwin immediately opened his mouth, welcoming Farley. Farley took the invitation and slipped his tongue inside, tasting his mate and smiling because he could tell Irwin had eaten candy. His mother had always forbidden him from eating any kind of sweet or chocolate, and now that she was losing her power over him, he was going a little nuts with all the things he wanted to experience.

Farley couldn't think of anything better than his mate tasting of candy, so he deepened the kiss. He couldn't believe this was his life and that he'd have it for decades to come. He'd panicked a bit when he'd realized Irwin was his mate the night of the party, but he shouldn't have. Like always, fate knew what they were doing. They'd placed Irwin in Farley's path at the exact moment in which Irwin needed him the most.

And maybe Farley had needed him, too, even though he hadn't realized it.

When Farley kissed Irwin, Irwin didn't resist. Why should he? He wanted to kiss his mate as much as Farley wanted to kiss him, and while he didn't understand why Farley felt that way, he didn't have to.

He trusted Farley not to lie to him. It wasn't always easy to accept what Farley said, but Irwin knew that he was working to make a better life for both of them. He wanted them to be happy together, and if he didn't think they would be if he moved in with Irwin right away, Irwin had to respect that. He didn't fully understand, but he didn't have to. His mate wanted this, and it was enough for Irwin to take a step back.

"We're going to be so happy together," Farley murmured. "But before we can be happy, you need to learn to be happy by yourself."

That made even less sense than the rest. Irwin had been by himself for a long time, yet he'd never been happy. On the other hand, he'd been happier since he'd met Farley than ever in his life. It wasn't just that his mother had been forced to stop hurting him. It was that Farley was showing him a future he'd never thought he'd have. Farley was showing him that he wouldn't have to be alone anymore, even though he had been for the first twenty-six years of his life.

Someone cleared their throat, and Irwin took a step away from Farley. He didn't go far and didn't stop touching his mate, but like this, the realtor wouldn't have to talk to one of their backs.

"I talked to your alpha," she said with a smile. "He agreed to pay for the apartment as long as you're sure it's what you want."

"It is." Irwin was tempted to look at Farley for confirmation, but maybe Farley was right, and it was time for him to start making decisions on his own.

Some people would see this like him not making decisions at all. His pride would pay for the apartment, not him. He couldn't afford anything like this because his mother had never allowed him to work. He didn't have anything to his name. Even the clothes he wore technically belonged to his mother because she'd bought them.

But this was what the pride did. The pride cared for its members, usually in the same house, but not always. Irwin would still be a pride member, even when he didn't live with them anymore. It made sense for Gal to want him to be on pride property. Irwin would find a way to give everything back. They hadn't given him much over the years, and he didn't care what most of them thought about him moving into an apartment paid for by Gal, but Gal was giving him everything he'd ever dreamed of, and Irwin felt he owed him.

"It'll take a few days for the paperwork to go through and everything, but I'm positive you'll be able to move in by the end of the week," the realtor promised. "If there's anything else you want to know or need, please call me."

Irwin felt a little dazed as she walked them back to the apartment's front door and then into the elevator. He had his own place. He would never have to live in his bedroom ever again, at least once he got the keys from the realtor. He was free from the house and from his mother.

Part of him still couldn't believe it. He suspected it would take a few days of him actually living in the apartment to finally relax, but that was okay. As long as he knew he'd never have to go back once he moved out, he'd be happy.

His mother wouldn't be. Eventually, she'd find out what was happening and try to stop it. Irwin hadn't seen her since Gal had talked to her, but he was sure she was planning something. That was how she was, and Irwin knew her well.

He still didn't know what Gal would do with her, and so far, he'd been too afraid to ask. Maybe it was time to get over that fear, but he didn't know if he could. He didn't truly want to find out what would happen to his mother. He just wanted her to leave him alone.

"Do you want me to take you back to the house?" Farley asked once they were outside.

Irwin looked up at the sky. It was cloudy and looked like it would rain later, but the day was dry for now. He wanted to take advantage of that. He'd been locked away in his bedroom and in the pride house for too long. Even though thick woods surrounded the house, he'd never been allowed to play there. It was too cold for him to strip down and shift, but that didn't mean he couldn't take a walk with a man he was falling in love with.

He squeezed Farley's hand. "Do we have to go now?"

"No. I don't have anything planned. I can stay with you for the rest of the day if you want me to."

"You never have to ask if I want you to spend the day with me. The answer is yes."

That made Farley laugh. Irwin was still stunned that he could get that kind of sound out of his mate. He wasn't even trying. He was being honest about how he felt and what he wanted, and for some reason, that seemed to delight Farley.

"I think we should spend the rest of the day together," Irwin agreed.

Farley raised their linked hands and pressed a kiss to the back of Irwin's. "Then we will. Do you have anything specific in mind?"

Irwin looked around. He hadn't been allowed to do anything like this in his life, and there were many things he wanted to try. He didn't want to be overwhelmed, especially because once he moved here, he'd have the opportunity to do whatever he wanted, anytime he wanted. He could explore Green Hill one day at a time.

His gaze landed on the coffee shop on the other side of the street. "How about we get one of those disgustingly sweet coffees you told me about, then take a walk in the park?"

Farley's smile softened. He looked at Irwin with so much adoration that Irwin almost glanced behind himself to check that he wasn't looking at someone else. It still didn't make sense to him that someone could stare at him like that, but he wanted to get used to it. He didn't want to doubt Farley's feelings for the rest of his life. He'd never been afraid that Farley would hurt him like his mother had, but sometimes, it was hard to understand that Farley truly wanted him.

"We can do that," Farley confirmed.

"That's what I want, then."

That, and possibly more kissing, but Irwin didn't want to push his luck. He already knew that Farley wanted him. There was no need for him to ask for reassurance every time a niggle of doubt made him freak out.

Hopefully, he'd get over feeling like this. He didn't understand why fate had chosen him for Farley, but he didn't need to understand. He was Farley's mate, and that was that. There didn't need to be a reason for it or an explanation. He was Farley's future, just like Farley was his.

And they were building a life together. It was everything Irwin could have hoped for and everything he hadn't allowed himself to dream about. It had been too painful, but he'd been wrong not to hope.

CHAPTER SIX

Irwin owned very little. Farley wasn't surprised, but he was incredibly angry at the sight of the two bags they'd filled. At twenty-six, Irwin should have clothes, books, and stuff he needed to pack to move, yet two bags was enough. Irwin didn't own books or anything like that. He didn't have anything precious to him that he didn't want to leave behind. He hadn't even wanted to return to pack once Gal bought the apartment. He'd wanted to stay there as soon as he got the keys, even though it was empty. It was as if he couldn't stand to be in the pride house one second longer, and Farley understood why more every time he visited.

What kind of person treated another human being — their son — like this? Farley hadn't asked, but he was pretty sure that the reason Irwin only owned a handful of things was his mother. Maybe she'd forbidden him to have more, or maybe Irwin had decided it would be safer because not having stuff meant she couldn't take it away from him. Either way, it was despicable, and Farley wanted to find her and yell at her the way she'd yelled at him.

"I can't believe I won't have to come back here ever again once we're done," Irwin said.

He'd become more talkative over the past few days, which was a delight. He was getting comfortable with Farley and the apartment, and Farley couldn't wait to see the kind of person he would grow into now that he was free. He knew he'd love Irwin no matter what, and it was good to watch him spread his wings and finally be allowed to live his life.

"You don't think you'll ever come back?" Farley asked

from his spot where he was sitting on the bed.

Irwin didn't hesitate at all before shaking his head. "Not to live—not unless I have to."

"And there won't be a reason for you to have to?"

"I guess it depends on Gal. He's my alpha, and if he tells me I need to move back in, I'll have to obey."

"He wouldn't do something like that." Farley tried to sound like he believed that, but what did he know?

He wasn't a shifter, and he'd never had a tribe. He wanted to believe that Gal would do whatever was best for his pride members, including Irwin, but how could he be sure?

He needed to have faith in his friends. They trusted Gal and were still pride members even after everything that had happened. That had to mean something. They understood much better than Farley what being part of a pride meant, so he needed to go with the flow.

"I don't think he would," Irwin agreed. "But you realize you're a pride member now, right?"

Farley blinked. "You and I aren't bonded."

"We don't need to be bonded. We just need to be mates, which we are. Besides, we're planning on bonding eventually."

It was true. It was too soon for them to even think about it, but it was in their future.

Apparently, the pride was in Farley's future, too.

He wasn't sure how to feel about that. He didn't want to have to obey the orders of a man he didn't know. At this point, he didn't even want to obey his parents' orders, and he did so only because he still lived under their roof. Did Gal really have that much authority over him? What did it mean?

Irwin sat beside Farley and put a hand on his thigh. "You don't have to worry about Gal. I know you don't trust him, but he won't do anything to us. He's a good person."

"I know." Farley hoped he sounded convincing.

Maybe not, given the way Irwin laughed.

"You'll get to know him in time."

"How? We won't be living here."

"But that doesn't change the fact that we belong to his pride. He's going to check in on us, things like that. You don't have to trust him. I'll trust him for both of us."

"Even though he didn't do anything to stop your mother?"

Irwin shrugged. "He didn't know. You didn't see what the pride was like before when the old alpha was still in charge. He knew what my mother was doing, and he didn't care. I think he believed she was controlling me for his sake. Maybe he thought that I wanted to take his place as the alpha, but I can't think of anything worse than being in charge of so many people. As long as I didn't give him trouble, he was happy to allow my mother to do whatever she wanted. Life wasn't good back then."

"It wasn't good recently, at least for you."

Farley was still angry and didn't think he would ever stop feeling that way. He understood what Irwin was saying, though. No matter how good a person Gal was, when he'd become the alpha, he had needed to learn everything about the pride and its members. He'd probably had so many problems to solve that he hadn't been able to see all of them, including the way Irwin's mother behaved. No one had told him, and he hadn't seen it, so how could he have done something about it?

A knock on the door interrupted the conversation. Irwin looked uneasy, so Farley got to his feet to open. If it was Irwin's mother or one of her friends, he'd act as a shield so Irwin wouldn't get hurt.

But it wasn't Irwin's mother. Simon, Jordan, and another guy stood on the other side of the door. Simon and the guy Farley didn't know appeared a bit hesitant, but Jordan didn't. He pushed past Farley before Farley could say anything, then made a beeline for Irwin. Farley started moving toward them, but he stopped when he saw Irwin smiling.

"We weren't sure we'd be able to catch you before you left," Jordan said as he leaned down to hug Irwin.

Irwin looked stunned, but he hugged Jordan back before getting to his feet. Things were a bit more hesitant with Simon and the other guy, but Irwin still appeared happy to see them, so Farley relaxed.

"I'm Farley, Irwin's mate," he said, introducing himself to the third guy.

The man nodded. "Ellery." He turned to Irwin. "I came to apologize for not seeing what was happening. If I had, I would have stepped in."

To Farley's surprise, Irwin hugged Ellery again. "I know you didn't know. After what you've gone through, I have no doubt that you would have tried to help me in any way you could. I don't blame you for not knowing." Irwin leaned back and looked at the others. "I don't blame any of you. I should have stood up to my mother and been stronger, but I wasn't, and that's on me."

Ellery shook his head. "You have no fault in this. It's all on your mother." He and Simon looked at each other. "Have you heard what's happening today?"

"No. What's going on?"

"Gal and the elders are talking to your mother. There's a good chance she'll be kicked out of the pride."

Ellery sounded sorry, but Farley doubted he was. He probably felt sorry for Irwin but not for his mother.

Farley quickly went to stand beside Irwin and pressed a hand against the small of his back. Irwin leaned against him, a little paler than he'd been before.

"You think she'll be exiled?"

"What she did was bad," Simon said. "Everyone is sorry that we didn't see it, but that's not the main problem. The main problem is that she hurt you for most of your life. She shouldn't have been allowed to do so, but more importantly, she shouldn't have *wanted* to do it. She did, and between that and everything else, I don't think Gal wants to keep her as a pride member."

Irwin slowly nodded. Farley didn't fully understand what they were talking about, but he could imagine it wasn't easy for a shifter to lose the pride they'd known all their life.

He couldn't think of a better punishment for Irwin's mother.

He shouldn't be happy that she'd be kicked out, but he didn't care. She'd hurt his mate in a way that would take years to heal from, and Farley wanted her to suffer.

"I want to talk to her before she leaves," Irwin declared.

Farley wasn't happy, but he also wasn't surprised. He suspected his mate needed closure. Maybe a small part of him still hoped that his mother would apologize. Farley doubted that would be the case, but he wouldn't stand in Irwin's way, even though he didn't want his mate to be unhappy.

The other three looked at each other, but thankfully, none of them tried to stop Irwin.

"I'll come with you," Farley said.

Irwin smiled at him. "I know. I couldn't do this without you, and you wouldn't let me talk to her alone. I want her to see how happy I am with you."

It looked like Irwin wanted to rub his happiness in his mother's face. Maybe that was what he needed after everything she'd put him through, and he'd come out happy and strong.

Good for him.

Irwin could tell Farley wasn't happy about his decision to talk to his mother. He wasn't, either. He couldn't think of anything worse than having to see his mother again, but he felt he needed to do this.

Once this was over, he'd be able to put a lid on his past and finally focus on his future. It was important to him, which was the only reason he wanted to see his mother today.

He didn't think she'd ever be sorry for what she did to him. If she could feel that way, she wouldn't have hurt him as much as she had. It wasn't only him, either. Over the years, she'd bullied many people in the pride, although not as badly as Irwin. He suspected that most pride members would be happy to see her go.

Kevin wouldn't be. Kevin would end up alone if Irwin's mother was forced to leave the pride. Those two had been best friends for as long as Irwin remembered, and while they had a few other people, they weren't close. They didn't behave in a way that made people want to be friends with them, but Irwin couldn't find it in himself to feel sorry. Kevin had hurt him almost as badly as his mother.

They were both getting what they deserved.

He and Farley walked down the hallway holding hands. Irwin knew he was squeezing a bit too hard, but Farley didn't say anything about it. He wasn't complaining about having to do this or about Irwin hurting him. He just wanted to be there for Irwin, something that had never happened before.

Irwin had always been on his own, but that was over. He'd never be alone again, and not only because he had Farley. Now that people were aware that Irwin had stayed away from them because he hadn't been allowed to make friends, they seemed to want to spend time with him and give him a chance. He was stunned, but he liked it, and he didn't want it to stop.

Jordan, Ellery, and Simon had promised that they could be friends even after Irwin moved out. Jordan and Simon lived in town, so they'd be able to see each other often. Ellery was still at the house, but he could understand what Irwin had gone through better than most people, and Irwin was excited at the thought of them growing closer.

He was excited about so many things these days. He'd never thought it possible, but for the first time, he was looking forward to seeing what the future would bring.

"You know you don't have to do this, right?" Farley suddenly said.

"I know."

"Do you think she'll apologize?"

"She might, just to show Gal that she's sorry, but I don't think he'll believe her. I certainly wouldn't. I don't think she's sorry for what she did to me, just that she was caught and that she's getting kicked out of the pride."

"How do you feel about that?"

Irwin took a moment to answer. "I think she deserves it. I think it wouldn't have happened if she hadn't hurt me, and I can't find it in myself to feel sorry for her."

"No one is going to blame you for not feeling sorry."

"I don't think so. I'm not happy about what's happening to her, but I can see she deserves it, and I'm not going to stand in Gal's way. He's the alpha and knows better than anyone how to punish his pride members."

Irwin wouldn't have felt this way if this had been the old alpha, but he trusted Gal. As soon as Gal had realized what was happening, he'd apologized and made amends. He'd done everything he could to make Irwin more comfortable, including finding him a therapist. Thanks to Gal, Irwin's path still wouldn't be easy, but it would be easier than it could have been. Irwin would always be thankful for that.

"I just don't want her to hurt you more than she already has," Farley grumbled.

Irwin squeezed his hand. "She'll try, but nothing she can say will hurt me. I've already heard all of it. I know that she'll tell me that I'm not worth anything, that you should have better than me, that I'll ruin your life and mine. I don't care about any of that because I know it's not the truth."

"You're stronger than I can ever be."

Irwin wasn't sure that was true, but it didn't matter. He didn't want Farley to have to be strong. He wanted his mate's life to be easy, and he'd make sure it was. From now on, he'd focus on his future and Farley.

When they reached Gal's office, they could hear voices behind the closed door. Normally, Simon would be there to tell Gal that someone was there to see him, but he'd stayed back with the others. He'd told Irwin that he didn't want anything to do with this. That wasn't a surprise, considering what had happened when Simon met his mate.

Thinking about it made Irwin angry. His mother and Kevin had tried running the life of too many people. Kevin wasn't going anywhere for now, but hopefully seeing what happened to Irwin's mother would be enough for him to realize he needed to stop being an asshole. If not, he'd eventually join her in exile.

Irwin knocked before Farley could ask him if he was sure this was the right thing to do again. The voices stopped, then footsteps came closer. The door opened, and Gal faced Irwin.

"Simon told you?" he asked.

Irwin nodded. "He did, and I want to be here."

Gal grimaced. "I'm not sure it's a good idea, but I won't stop you if you feel you need to do this. Just be warned that it's not going to be easy."

"I didn't expect it to be."

Gal stared at Irwin for a moment before stepping to the side and letting him and Farley in.

Irwin swallowed and walked into the room. He wasn't surprised to see the pride's beta was there, along with the pride elders. His gaze zeroed in on his mother, though.

She was sitting in front of Gal's desk, with the other chairs placed in a semi-circle around her so that everyone could see her. She was right smack in the middle, with her head bowed and her fingers linked together in her lap. She was trying hard to appear weak and repentant, but when she looked up, Irwin could see that she wasn't sorry. Her expression was arrogant, and when she saw him, she narrowed her eyes and started getting up.

"Stay where you are," Gal ordered as he closed the door and went back to sit behind his desk. "Your son's presence doesn't change what's happening. You won't talk to him or attempt to hurt him in any way."

"Of course not," she said in a meek voice. "Why would I hurt my son?"

Irwin almost rolled his eyes. Why would she hurt her son, indeed.

There were no empty chairs left, so he and Farley leaned against the wall as far away as possible from her. Farley wrapped an arm around Irwin's shoulders as if to shield him, and Irwin leaned against him, grateful for the support.

"Where were we?" one of the elders, Helga, asked.

"I was explaining that I had a hard time getting used to Gal becoming our alpha," Irwin's mother quickly said. "There have been so many changes, and it wasn't easy. I might have taken my anger out on my son, and I shouldn't have, but I never meant to hurt him." She hesitated. "I also wasn't sure how to react when I found out about his mate. He's not a tiger shifter. He's not a shifter at all, and he doesn't understand our ways. I don't want my son to be hurt or unhappy, which is why I tried to intervene. It was for my son's happiness, nothing more."

Irwin had to resist the urge to snort. Did she really believe she was fooling anyone? The elders knew her. They'd seen how she behaved most of Irwin's life. At least some of them had to have known what was happening to him. He was angry they hadn't intervened, but that didn't matter right now.

"Trying to stop two mates from being together goes against the council's laws," Gal said. "As for you getting used to me being the alpha, I don't see what the problem is. I've been treating your people better than your old alpha ever did. What was there to get used to? Having fair rules for everyone? Losing your power over your fellow pride members?"

The expression on Irwin's mother's face turned to rage. "You ruined everything when you became alpha."

"Did I?" Gal didn't sound offended but curious.

"You put people in charge who never should have been. Now you're trying to take my son from me, and you're going to ruin every chance at a happy future he might have."

"You already did that on your own," Irwin snapped. He wouldn't allow his mother to lie, even though it meant standing up to her. He was finally ready to do so.

Farley sucked in a breath but didn't try to stop Irwin from confronting his mother. He wasn't surprised Irwin had finally gone off. Farley had had enough, and he'd only spoken to her a few times. He could only imagine how Irwin felt.

Farley wasn't going to step in, but he'd be there for Irwin. He unwrapped his arm from around Irwin's shoulders to give him more freedom to move, but he took his hand instead so they wouldn't be separated. Irwin needed to feel Farley's support, and Farley was ready for it.

The way Irwin's mother stared at them was enough to tell Farley how angry she was that they were mates. He grinned, knowing it would piss her off. Sure enough, she looked like she wanted to strangle him, but instead of scaring him, it made him smile even wider.

"How can you say that?" she asked, turning her attention

to Irwin. "I've only tried to do the best for you."

"You wouldn't know the best for me even if it slapped you in the face," Irwin answered.

Farley was impressed. His mate had always been meek, and Farley hadn't expected him to stand up to his mother like this.

He loved it.

Irwin had come a long way from the man he was the night of the party, and Farley couldn't have been prouder of him. He understood that their future would be complicated and hard, that Irwin still had many things to work on, but he felt that confronting Irwin's mother was the first step toward that. Irwin was freeing himself of her, finally letting her control go, and it was so good to see. Maybe coming here today was the right decision. Irwin felt stronger because of it, and that was all Farley wanted.

"You've made my life hell," Irwin continued. "You controlled me in every aspect of it. You told me what I could eat and when, who I could talk to, and who I should stay away from. You forbid me from being part of pride life, and when I didn't obey your orders, you hurt me physically. I'll never forgive you for any of it, and I needed you to see how strong I am even after everything you've done to make me weak."

Irwin squared his shoulders. He didn't let go of Farley's hand, but he didn't have to in order to look impressive. Farley wasn't the only one to think so. Gal was nodding as Irwin spoke, while the elder who had spoken earlier was smiling.

"You're everything that's wrong with the pride," Irwin continued. "You behaved like a bully with everyone, but you specifically targeted the weakest of us, like me. You and Kevin have done unimaginable harm, and it's time to stop. I've never felt happier than I am now, and I would never have had this if I hadn't found the strength to get away from you."

"You ungrateful little—"

"Thank you, Irwin," Gal interjected before Irwin's mother could start insulting him. "I'm glad you felt strong enough to tell us about your mother's behavior and the way she treated you. I'm sorry this happened and that we allowed it to continue for so long."

"It's all right. It's over now, and I'm happy."

"You have no right to do any of this," Irwin's mother screamed. "This is my home. I was born in this house, and you can't kick me out. It belongs to me as much as it belongs to any other pride member and much more than it belongs to you. You're a stranger. You don't belong here."

Gal didn't look impressed by her ranting. He also didn't look like he cared, which made Farley grin.

It was good to see her finally get what she deserved. Farley had no doubt that if she could, she'd hurt someone else, but for the near future, she'd be alone. He wasn't sure how it worked when a pride member was kicked out, but he imagined she'd have to find a new place to live, and she might even have to leave Green Hill. He hoped that would be the case. He didn't want Irwin to have to see her ever again after today.

"Gal is our alpha," the elder who had smiled at Irwin before said.

Gal nodded. "Thank you, Helga."

She waved his words away. "It doesn't matter how you became the alpha. You are, and we've accepted you. Everyone agrees that life has become better since you've taken charge. It's a fact that only a fool wouldn't see."

"You can't do this to me," Irwin's mother begged.

It was as if she'd finally realized that she wouldn't win. She would try to look like a victim now to get pity from the elders and convince them not to kick her out. Hopefully, they'd see her behavior for what it was.

The way she spoke made Farley's skin crawl. She was a manipulator and had been all of her life. That wasn't going to change, which meant that the only way for the pride to be safe from her was to kick her out. Luckily, the elders and Gal seemed to be on board with that.

"You've been a pride member your entire life," another elder said. "You were given every opportunity to be a good person and a productive member of this pride. You were given a home, food, and respect. Instead of behaving the way any good pride member should have, you hurt people. It's over, Anne. You should never have treated your son the way you did, and the fact that you don't seem one bit sorry means that you don't have a place with us."

"This isn't over," Irwin's mother snapped. "I'll go to the council. They'll see that my place is here."

"You can contact them," Gal said easily. "I'm sure they'll be interested in knowing that you were trying to come between two mates."

"I hate you," Irwin's mother spat out as she got to her feet.

For a moment, Farley wondered if she was going to attack Gal or worse, Irwin. He was ready to put himself in front of his mate and keep him safe if he needed to, but thankfully, she seemed to realize that attacking anyone in the room would only make her case worse. If she did that, Gal would be in his right to call the enforcers and have her taken away.

"I think everyone here agrees that we don't want you as a pride member anymore," Gal continued. "You'll be given a few hours to pack your things and take as many of them as possible. I can't force you to leave Green Hill, but you won't be allowed in pride territory anymore." He leaned over his desk. "And if I learn that you've tried going anywhere near your son, I'll make sure you're never allowed to set foot in town ever again. You're not a pride member anymore, but he is, and I protect my people."

She screamed again, rage and hatred pouring out of her. It made Farley shiver and be glad that he wasn't the main focus of those feelings, but being Irwin's mate meant that he might have to deal with her eventually. He wouldn't be surprised if she decided to stick around.

If she ever attempted to get to Irwin, Farley would make sure Gal knew about it.

"Please," she said, visibly trying to calm herself. "I've never had another home. My place is here."

Gal ignored her. The man Farley knew was the pride's beta stood up and stepped closer to Irwin's mother. Irwin didn't need to watch her be taken away, so Farley hugged him. Irwin slumped against Farley's chest, wrapping his arms around him and holding on to him. Farley was pretty sure he was trying to ignore his mother's ranting and screaming, and hopefully, he wouldn't let her words get to him.

None of what she did or thought mattered. She was gone, and all of this was over.

Irwin was pretty sure he'd always love his mother, or rather, the idea of what his mother should have been. She'd given birth to him and had raised him in a pride that had been less than ideal, and maybe in the beginning, she'd done what she could to be a good mother. As far as Irwin could remember, though, she'd always tried to control him. She'd had years to realize that it was wrong and try to change her behavior, but instead, it had become worse, and Irwin was glad all of this was finally over.

He wouldn't miss her. He would miss the kind of person she should have been, but that was okay. He was finally free and ready to live his life, even though he wouldn't have his mother anymore.

Forest took her away, and the elders started leaving the room. Gregory nodded at Irwin on his way out while Helga stopped and hugged him hard. He hugged her back, unsure what was happening but needing it.

"I am so very sorry for what happened to you," Helga murmured. "I didn't know it was that bad, but even so, I should have stepped in. You don't deserve any of what she did to you."

Irwin didn't want to cry, but it was hard. "It's all right. I don't want to resent anyone or be angry. I don't want to be like her."

"You never could be. Your heart is too good for you to be like your mother."

Irwin prayed Helga was right. He didn't know what had happened to his mother to turn her into the bitter, controlling woman she'd become, but he never wanted to be anything like her.

Eventually Helga left, too, and Farley and Irwin were alone with Gal. The alpha looked tired, and Irwin felt guilty. It was his fault Gal had to kick out a member of the pride. His mother had been in charge of the kitchen, and it probably wouldn't be easy to find someone to take her place.

"I could take charge of the kitchen for a while," he offered. "I'm not a great cook, but I don't want the pride to be in trouble because you had to kick my mother out."

Gal shook his head right away. "I don't want you to have to stay when it's clear you're ready to leave. I'll find a way to make it work, don't worry. You go out there and live your life."

He rose from his chair and walked around the desk. Irwin wasn't sure what made him do it, but he threw himself into Gal's arms and hugged him hard.

Gal looked startled, but as soon as Irwin landed against his chest, he wrapped his arms around him.

This man would always be in Irwin's life. He was Irwin's alpha, and he'd shown that he wanted the best for Irwin and the rest of the pride.

"I'm proud to call you my alpha," Irwin murmured.

"And I'm proud to call you my pride member. Go and be happy, Irwin. You deserve it."

Irwin nodded, and even though he didn't want to cry, a tear rolled from his eye and down his cheek. Gal was incredibly gentle as he dried it.

Irwin reached back for Farley, and his mate was there right away. He linked their fingers together, and Irwin could tell he was more than ready to go. That was a good thing, because he was, too.

He turned to Farley. "Let's go home."

Farley nodded. He said goodbye to Gal and dragged Irwin out of the office. They went back to Irwin's room to take his things, then left the house in which Irwin had been so unhappy.

He'd be back eventually. He was still a pride member and belonged here as much as the pride members who lived here. For now, though, he was free of this place and of his mother, and he could feel the weight of it lifting from his shoulders.

The past was over. His future was holding his hand, and Irwin went along willingly.

They shimmered straight into the apartment. It was still a mess of new furniture and boxes of stuff, but Irwin would have time to find a place for everything later. Right now, he needed his mate, and he had him.

They dropped Irwin's bags on the floor, and Farley dragged Irwin to the couch. It was new and as soft as a cloud, and as Irwin sat, he closed his eyes and allowed himself to breathe.

It would take some time to wrap his mind around his new life, but he could do it. Besides, he wasn't doing it alone. He had Farley and their friends, so he'd be fine.

He and Farley sat on the couch for the rest of the afternoon, watching TV and cuddling as if nothing else in the world mattered. As far as Irwin was concerned, that was true. For today, the world outside the apartment didn't exist. He had everything he wanted here, and he'd never been happier.

He was starting to get hungry when someone knocked on the door. He looked at Farley with wide eyes, not knowing what to do. "I'm not expecting anyone," he said.

"Do you want me to open it?"

The way Farley smiled told Irwin he knew who was there. That meant it was safe, and Irwin was glad to know that. Eventually, he would accept that everything was safe in his new life and that he didn't have to be afraid to open a door or do something his mother would have forbidden him to do before.

He jumped to his feet. "I'll get it. It's my apartment, right?"

Farley grinned. "It is."

Irwin didn't have to go far to reach the front door, since it opened in his living room. He grinned when he saw who was in the hallway.

"How did you know I was hungry?" he asked Jordan.

Jordan grinned back. "Farley texted me that he could hear your stomach growl."

"And he told you to bring pizza?"

"No, that was my suggestion," Nestor, Jordan's mate, said. "I thought we could spend some time with you and celebrate your new apartment. I texted Simon, and he said that he and his mate are coming. They'll be bringing more food and drinks."

Irwin's smile was so wide it hurt his cheeks, but he didn't care. He loved this. It wasn't a housewarming party, but it was what he needed.

He had *everything* he needed — his mate, a new apartment, and friends. He'd have to find a job, but while the thought was intimidating, he couldn't wait and was looking forward to it. He'd never dreamed of being so independent, but it felt good, especially knowing that even if he failed, he had people who cared about him and who would catch him when he fell. He'd been alone before, even though he'd lived with the rest of the pride in the pride house. Now that he lived by himself, he'd never be alone anyway. The people who cared about him would be there to support him.

It wouldn't be easy, but he didn't need it to be.

He sat next to Farley on the couch, and Farley wrapped an arm around his shoulders. Eventually, Simon and his mate arrived, and they set out to eat. Irwin's heart felt like it was about to explode. It felt bigger than just a few weeks ago when he'd still been trapped at the pride house.

"Everything okay?" Farley asked in a whisper.

Irwin nodded and leaned closer to him. "It's a lot, but I love it."

Farley kissed Irwin's temple. "You deserve all of this. You deserve to be happy and have everything you can ever want in your life."

"I already have it."

"Guys, less kissing and more eating," Jordan teased.

Irwin's cheeks flushed, but he laughed. "Are you going to eat all of it if I don't hurry?"

"Damn right, I will. There aren't any pizza leftovers in my life."

Irwin snatched another slice. "Then I'd better hurry."

His chest hurt in the best of ways. He wouldn't have any of this if he hadn't met Farley, but he had, and he could never thank fate enough for that. By giving him his mate, it had opened his life to a happiness he'd never expected to have, and while he didn't know how to deal with how overwhelming all of it was, he didn't have to do it tonight.

Tonight, he just had to be himself. His friends and Farley loved him just the way he was, and eventually, he'd learn to love himself the same way.

CHAPTER SEVEN

Farley woke up to the sensation of someone rubbing against him. He wasn't used to it yet, but the thought that he and Irwin would get to have this for decades to come made him smile.

Then Irwin made him moan.

He pushed his ass harder against Farley's groin. Farley tightened his arms around him so he wouldn't even think about sneaking out of bed, and he squeaked as if he hadn't expected Farley to be awake.

"How do you expect me to stay asleep when you're doing that?" he asked before kissing Irwin's neck.

"I didn't mean to wake you up."

"Then you shouldn't have done that."

They barely knew each other, but at the same time, Farley felt he knew all the important things about his mate. They were still far from being ready to bond or move in together, but Farley loved their sleepovers and waking up with Irwin in his arms. Even though Irwin was slightly bigger, that was how he wanted to sleep, and Farley would never deny him what he needed.

"I'm sorry," Irwin murmured.

"I'm not."

Farley rolled Irwin to his back, then to his other side so they faced each other. He didn't like the way Irwin always seemed to be waiting for the moment Farley would reject him, but he wasn't surprised that was how his mate felt. He'd been rejected by his mother and by most of the pride, and even though a lot of the members were trying to make amends now, the wounds were deep and still too fresh.

Irwin hadn't gone back since he'd moved out, and Farley didn't think he would any time soon. He needed time and space to heal, and his apartment gave him that and the freedom he'd never had. It also gave them a place where they could be together without worrying that someone would walk in on them, which was why Farley spent several nights a week there. He might not have moved in, but that didn't mean he was staying away.

Irwin's gaze jumped away from Farley.

Farley was getting used to how skittish Irwin was. He didn't like it, but only time would change Irwin's behavior. He'd started talking to a therapist, and Farley hoped it would help him further. He hated feeling powerless to help Irwin, but he was only a nineteen-year-old guy who had no idea what he was doing.

But when they were like this, everything felt right. They didn't have to worry about the world outside of the apartment. The only thing that mattered was them.

Farley kissed Irwin, smiling when his mate moaned. He was always so responsive that it was impossible for Farley to wonder if Irwin enjoyed what they were doing. He couldn't hide that he did. Every time Farley kissed him, he pressed closer and demanded more, and Farley was delighted to give all of that to him. He'd give him so much more if he could, but for now, this was enough.

Irwin clung to Farley as if he never wanted to let him go. Farley felt the same, and as they kissed, he tried to prove it to his mate. He caressed every inch of his mate's skin and cherished every single touch. Irwin wouldn't let him stop kissing him, but that was okay. Farley didn't need to in order to bring pleasure to his mate.

He slid his hands down Irwin's naked back to the elastic

band of his underwear. Irwin was still too shy to sleep naked with Farley, and he blushed every time Farley came to bed without clothes on. It was adorable, although Farley had never said it out loud. He didn't want Irwin to think he was making fun of him. At the moment, he didn't want Irwin to think at all. It was too easy for him to get lost in his thoughts and disappear inside his head.

Irwin squeaked again when Farley cupped his ass with both hands. Farley kissed him harder as he slid the fabric down, leaving it around Irwin's thighs. He rubbed his palms over Irwin's ass again, gently separating the cheeks but not daring to explore that area yet. Irwin had blushed so hard the first time he had, Farley had been sure he was about to combust. They needed to talk about it and about what they both expected, but not this morning.

Farley let go of Irwin's ass to finish pushing down his underwear. He could feel Irwin's skin heat under his touch, and he was tempted to lean back to look at him and check if he was as red as expected, but Irwin wouldn't like that, so he didn't. Eventually, Irwin would learn not to be self-conscious with Farley, and Farley couldn't wait.

Irwin moaned when their cocks touched each other. He snuggled closer, making a satisfied sound when Farley wrapped his arms around him and held him close. Irwin always loved that, maybe because he was touch-starved. His mother had never been a hugging person, and Irwin's father died when he was a child. Most people had stayed away from him so Anne wouldn't freak out, and those who hadn't had been as nasty as her and would never have hugged a child. Farley's heart wept for the child Irwin had been, and while he couldn't change the past, he could make sure that Irwin's future would be happy.

He wouldn't have it any other way.

They rutted against each other. Farley was used to doing

more with the few guys he'd slept with, but with Irwin, this felt perfect. There was no rush and no need to get anywhere faster. As long as Irwin was comfortable and falling apart in Farley's arms, Farley was happy, and he hoped his mate was, too.

When Farley rolled them so that Irwin was under him, Irwin clung to him as if he was planning to never let go. Farley would be happy because no matter what had happened in the past, it didn't matter. Their future wouldn't be easy, but he didn't need easy. He just needed Irwin.

He had him.

Irwin's body stiffened when he came. Farley kept him cradled against his chest, their lips still pressed together even though they weren't kissing anymore. They breathed against each other's mouths, their breaths mingling as their bodies tangled together and their release mixed between their bodies. Farley almost couldn't believe he'd come like this, but everything about Irwin delighted him. He felt he'd always want more but that, at the same time, whatever Irwin was willing to give him would be enough.

Farley stopped moving when things became too sensitive. He didn't want to let go of his mate, though, so he didn't. He blindly grabbed the underwear he'd slid off Irwin earlier and used that to clean them as well as he could. It wasn't great, but he wasn't ready to leave the bed yet and suspected he wasn't the only one. Irwin was plastered against his side, looking like he was planning to stay there for the rest of his life, or at the very least, for a few more hours.

Farley could think of nothing better.

He stretched out against the pillow and kissed the top of Irwin's head. Irwin wiggled as if uncomfortable, but Farley didn't think he was. He always had to be careful, though. Irwin wasn't used to standing up for himself or saying out loud what he liked and didn't like, and it would be too easy to do or make him do things he wasn't up to. Farley never wanted to do that. Bonding would make things easier because he'd be able to feel what Irwin felt, but neither of them was ready for that.

Irwin needed to learn how to be on his own, while Farley had to find a path for his life. There was no hurry because they both had a good support system. Farley had always had it, but Irwin had just discovered his, and he needed to get to know them better and learn to trust them. Farley would be by his side whenever he needed him, but Irwin would have to do a lot of this on his own.

He could do it. Farley had faith in him.

ABOUT THE AUTHOR

Catherine is the creator of several series, most of them paranormal, including the Whitedell Pride Series and the Gillham Pack Series. While she graduated in translation, she decided to go the writer's way because it was more fun to create her own stories and characters.

She's been living in Italy for more than twenty years, but she's a daughter of the North—Belgium to be precise—and she misses it so much that she's already planning to move back.

She loves pizza—probably too much—her son, her pets, and of course, books. She sneaks some reading time into her schedule every time she has five minutes free from writing, demands from her various pets and son, and lastly, housework.

Connect with her:

lievens.catherine@gmail.com
BookBub: https://www.bookbub.com/authors/catherine-lievens
Website: https://authorcatherinelievens.com/
Facebook: https://www.facebook.com/catherine.lievens.9
Facebook Group: https://www.facebook.com/groups/411788002341528/
Twitter: https://twitter.com/authorCLievens
Newsletter: http://eepurl.com/c-uvKn

www.ingramcontent.com/pod-product-compliance
Lightning Source LLC
Chambersburg PA
CBHW060646130626
46555CB00002B/980